I actually heard the ripping sound of my own throat, saw my crimson blood splattering into his snow-white face. I fell backwards and stared through the glass into space. I knew I wasn't coming back. Oddly, I didn't care that I was dying. I stared into Sydney Vale's black eyes, noticing a glimmer of light in their murky depths, a dim shimmering over the blackness. He squeezed my arm, a final gesture before I went to the other side.

I turn away from a friend I once loved and look through the window. Stars twinkle in my dying eyes, oscillate to the shallow beating of my heart as blood soaks my shirt. Remembering all I have lost, countless friends who died for nothing, I notice Syd's moon-like face reflected on the glass, a dim milky gleam on an endless black canvas. The glowing red eye in the center of his head throbs like a heart among the stars. I look past his reflection—Syd's sharp breathing the only sound—and let my gaze drift into the immense darkness of space.

DELIGHTFUL AGONY

BY DAVID WHITMAN

CONTENTS

A BETTER WORLD

THE CITY OF CARVERTON — VICTORIAN ERA

She was just a street whore, Simon thought, watching the rain strike his window. Lightning flashed brilliantly outside, illuminating his cluttered room in a short burst of effulgent light. He watched the shadows flicker and dance across the wall and let his gaze return to the howling storm.

He had been obsessing about Mina O'Connor for the last few weeks to the point of madness. It was not hard to imagine her angelic eyes—hypnotic and penetrating, the sort of eyes one could quite easily get lost inside for days. Mina would always gaze up at Simon when she was pleasuring him, never letting their stare unlock. Her black hair was cut shorter than was the style and the curls tickled just around her doll-like face like the petals of an ebony rose. She would watch him as he exploded into orgasm, her piercing eyes never leaving his face. Normally, he would feel uncomfortable at such intimacy—but he would always stare right back as he came, falling into her green eyes like they were blistering tunnels into her soul.

A few times Simon had even taken her to his home and made tea, enjoying the conversation much more than he was willing to admit. Though she was only twenty years old, she was very well read in most everything, an attribute that he found charming. Mina, a street whore, had more education than most of his pseudo-intellectual friends. She had left her unloving parents only two years ago hoping to find some work in the big city as an actress. Her dreams soon crushed by the harsh realities of the city, she found herself selling her body in order to survive.

"I just want things to be better," Mina had whispered, sipping her tea methodically by the fireplace, her moist eyes lost within her own dreams. "There must be a better world."

"There is, Mina," Simon had said, genuinely meaning his words. "And someday you will be there."

The night Simon saw her corpse still played in his mind daily. Mina did not show up at their appointed meeting place—a trash scattered alley near the end of town. After about thirty minutes of waiting in the shadows, he decided to walk home, his head low under his hat so that he would not be recognized frequenting such a seedy section of town. When he noticed the night watchmen gathering just down the street, he attempted to cross to the other side.

"You there!" an officer had shouted. "Come here!"

Reluctantly, Simon approached the suspicious group.

Mina lay on the ground before the street lamp—throat cut in a jagged gash, congealed blood surrounding her waif-like body in a thick, crimson puddle. She stared upwards to the night sky, skin glistening around the eyes where her final tears had fallen. Her mouth was open slightly, frozen in a final sigh. White teeth, speckled with blood, could be seen peeking out underneath her full lips.

Simon did not even know that he was crying until a teardrop fell from the bottom of his chin. A sob escaped from his lips and he barely managed to contain it.

At that moment, he knew that he had loved Mina O'Connor, *despite everything* that she was.

"You, sir," The night watchman said, his furry eyebrows arching inquisitively. "Do you know this woman? Do you know her name?"

Simon stared at the man, momentarily too stunned to speak. He wiped the tears away and said, "No, I do not. I've never seen her in my life."

"Why are you crying, then?" the man asked suspiciously. "We care not if you frequent the prostitutes around here, my good man. We merely want to identify this poor woman."

"I do not know her. I was weeping because she is so young. No one deserves such a death."After a few other questions,

Simon excused himself. It was not until he got back to his flat that he realized what he had done. In order to protect his limited standing in society, he had not identified the name of one of the most important people he had ever met.

Simon learned from the newspaper that the local church had buried Mina in Dark Hollow Cemetery with an unmarked tombstone. It was not often that the church did such a thing, but the fact that she was but a young girl, and that she was murdered so violently, must have touched something in the parishioners.

"I should have told them her name," Simon said, staring into the glowing flames of the fireplace as he sipped his tea. His best friend, Oscar Riley, was sitting just across from him, lighting up his pipe as he nodded.

"Yes," Oscar said, inhaling deeply of the smoke. "You should have."

"I'm evil."

"Yes, you are," Oscar shot back, grinning wickedly. Pipe smoke trailed from his long nose, giving him the appearance of a demon possessed in the shadowy sparkle of the fireplace.

Simon sighed and finished off the rest of his wine, swallowing the crimson liquid like it was arsenic. "I'm so glad that I asked you to come over and help me feel better."

"You know it is my nature, my friend. If one wants to hear something easy, one does not come to me. The simple fact is that this poor young lady is lying in that cemetery without a name. You could have prevented that. As…skilled as she was at her art, she deserves better. She was so young."

"I know," Simon said, closing his eyes as if it pained him to see. "And you are right. She was a very special girl."

Oscar chuckled, shaking his head like he had heard a bad joke.

Simon frowned. "What is funny?"

"She was not merely special, Simon. You were falling in love with her. You *were* in love with her. It is probably safe to assume that you would have rescued her from the…unfortunate lifestyle had she not been murdered. There is a way to correct this, my friend."

"Yes, I should tell the church her name."

"Indeed. Of course…"

"What?"

"You will then probably be looked at as a murder suspect." Oscar grinned again, the smile stretching the sides of his face to comical proportions.

"Will you do me a favor?" Simon asked.

"You know I will."

"Will you go with me to Dark Hollow?"

"Well, I can't go tomorrow morning—but I should be able to go with you some time in the late afternoon."

"I do not mean tomorrow. I mean now."

Oscar snickered. "I suppose. Do you realize how suspicious it will look standing over a murdered girl's grave after dark? What could you possibly want to do there now?"

"I want to apologize to her. I need to. I will go to the church tomorrow morning and tell them her real name."

An hour later, they stood before the gates of Dark Hollow, the chill wind ruffling gently through their coats. Leafless trees stabbed defiantly into the sky, the branches reaching up toward the full moon. The arched gateway, double angels flanking each side, appeared to Simon like the dreaded opening to a part of his guilty mind that he would rather let sleep. The tombstones beyond the gate glowed softly in the moonlight. It was unnaturally quiet. Not even a cricket chirped.

"Do you even know where the grave is, Simon?" Oscar whispered. His voice had lost its humorous edge, replaced by a somber, respectful tone.

"Yes. I watched them bury her from the gate. It's off to the left there." Simon was already through the archway when he realized that Oscar was not following him. "You coming?"

"No, I'd rather wait. I'll be able to see you from here. It's more considerate, I think. I did not even know Miss O'Connor. It's a bit creepy here as well. A man by the name of Jacob Atherton committed suicide back in the fall here. Hanged himself from a tree."

Simon nodded and continued his walk through the jutting tombstones. The thought that he was stepping over the corpses of the dead was quite unnerving. He had never believed in ghosts, but there was something about being in a graveyard near the midnight hour that brought out the child in him.

When he got to Mina's tombstone, he turned around to see his friend. Oscar was still by the gate, his pipe glowing in the foggy darkness.

"I am so sorry, Mina," Simon whispered, staring down at the earth as if he could see her face. Thinking of her buried underneath his feet made him ill. It seemed so wrong that so much beauty could be corrupted by decay.

A faint ethereal giggling cleaved through the thick air. For a brief moment, the air shimmered before him in shadows and stars.

Mina's petite figure stood before him, her head cocking curiously to the side before she vanished. It was a mannerism she often did, as if she wanted to study him like a painting she could not quite figure out.

The button in his pants popped open, and he felt a cold sensation trail up his thigh and around his hip. The icy fingers dragged upwards and under his shirt. He felt Mina's frosty hands caress around his chest before retreating back down and into his pants. Despite his fear, Simon felt himself becoming aroused.

Frozen water enveloped the head of his member as the ghost tasted him, her icicle-like fingers trailing lovingly over his shivering stomach. She stayed like that for a few seconds, her cadaverous mouth over the head, before taking him all the way inside.

Simon gasped, both repulsed and stimulated by the feeling. The skin on his member was moving up and down as phantom lips pulled at the flesh, a slimy substance glistening in the moonlight. He moaned, blood rushing through his body in an explosive blast.

His semen hung in the air where her mouth would be, then fell to the soil below where it landed with a sizzle before disappearing into the earth.

Mina giggled, a chilly hissing of air blasting into his wet crotch.

Simon stared down at the ground, too stunned to move,

his breath firing from his lips in short staccato blasts. An oily substance covered his member, burning his skin. He rubbed it away in revulsion, wiping it on his jacket.

Buttoning up his pants, Simon walked from the tombstone in a dazed trance, his eyes blank as he exited the archway. He promptly leaned against the wall; eyes closed on his sweat-drenched face.

Oscar put his hand on his friend's arm. "Simon? What's wrong? Are you ill?"

Simon shuddered. "Oscar, I do not know how to say this."

"You're not going to tell me you saw her ghost?

"She took me in her mouth," Simon whispered, falling to his knees.

"I don't understand."

Simon stared at his friend, the moonlight giving the sweat on his face a luminescent sheen. "Just like I said, Oscar. She took me in her mouth."

Oscar frowned. "I think we should take you home."

An hour later, Simon sat shivering before the fireplace, a steaming cup of tea in his hands, his dark hair still wet from his scalding bath. He had told the entire tale to Oscar. They had even examined the slime-like residue from his privates—it was green and smelled of damp soil and rotting meat.

"I'm still not sure what happened out there," Oscar said, yawning.

"You don't believe me?" Simon asked, placing his teacup down on the table.

"I didn't say that, Simon. It's very possible that you dreamed the whole thing. You've been very guilty—losing sleep. It's easy to see how this can happen."

"Are you saying I pleasured myself over Mina's grave, Oscar?" Simon asked, his eyes haunted by the glow of the fire. "That I rubbed the dirt of her grave upon myself? Do you really think I am that mad? That I am that sick?"

"I can tell by looking at your face that you think it is possible. I'm only telling you what you already think."

Simon put his fingers over his face. "God. I'm a step away from the madhouse."

Oscar sighed. "Your insanity is understandable, my friend. You lost someone you loved. She was brutally ripped from your life. Added onto that are all the other things, such as your guilt. It's perfectly understandable that you imagined a graveyard sex act over her body." An amoral grin came over his face. "Was it good?"

Simon peeked through his fingers, his eyes wide, though there was the hint of a smile on his face. "You are not asking what I think you are asking?"

Oscar laughed righteously. "Of course I am. Let's just say it was true—which we have no way of proving anyway. It is not every day you get a sexual act from a ghost. So...was it good, my friend?"

Simon sighed through his grin. "You are even more insane than I am. I guess it was good...though it was repulsive, too. I was too scared to truly enjoy it. It felt...wrong, you know? It was cold. It was as if I had thrust my member into a handful of melting snow. Dear Lord, I cannot believe I am talking about this."

Oscar slapped Simon affectionately on the shoulder. "Why not? We've been friends since childhood, have we not? We tell each other everything." He got up and stretched. "I'm afraid I must leave. I'll stop by tomorrow and see how you are doing."

"Thanks for being here with me, Oscar."

"No problem at all." Oscar turned back to face his friend. "Oh and did you drop some coins?"

"Eh? What do you mean?"

"I hoped you dropped some coins on her grave. You can't go around taking such things for free from prostitutes. It is bad manners."

Simon groaned, a large smile on his face. "Oh, God! Get out!"

"Why is everyone always telling me that?" Oscar asked, opening the door with a grin.

Simon dreamed of Mina that night.

He was on a boat in the center of the lake near the cemetery. The sky was dark—the stars glimmering down onto the undulating surface of the black water, the cool wind rustling through his wavy hair. The boat rocked underneath his weight. The full moon gave his surroundings a bluish glow.

He could see a child's pallid face just underneath the water, her hair flowing around her head like a dream. Though the child was only about four, he sensed instinctively that it was Mina. She smiled, her tiny mouth opening widely, bubbles floating to the surface and popping audibly into the cool air. Beyond her teeth, he could see nothing but blackness. Her eyes were dark as well, standing out in deep contrast to the cloud-white flesh of her face—ebony windows into her dead soul. The child rose up from the lake, her porcelain visage breaking through with a wet shriek. Though the smile stayed on her face, she continued to scream, steam rising from her mouth and into the glittering stars above.

She was hovering above the boat, the water falling from her feet and into the lake like soft rain, a white dress clinging to her gaunt form. Her ebony hair clung to the side of her cheeks in straight lines, giving the appearance that her chalky face was some kind of perverse flower.

Mina outstretched her miniscule arms in a crucifixion pose, her screams filling the air like a watery aria. She stopped screaming, thick black water running from her open mouth like blood. Her eyes narrowed, head turning to the side characteristically. The water dripping from her decomposing feet and into the lake was the only sound.

They studied each other quietly in the moonlight.

"I thought we had more, Simon," Mina finally said, her voice low and wet. "I was nothing but your whore."

Simon sobbed. "We did, Mina. I lost my nerve. When I saw you, I was so stunned I was not thinking clearly. I really do love you."

Mina put her drenched hand to her face, but not before a misty giggle shot from her full lips. "I wanted too much to be more than just your whore, Simon. You have no idea how much I adored you. How much I loved you."

Simon held out his hand. "I love you, too. I would do anything to change what happened. Anything to bring you back."

Mina offered an odd smile, water pouring from her teeth and down her chin. "You need to go to my grave, Simon. You need to go into my coffin. There is something there for you— something for us."

"I promise I will."

She touched his hand as she descended back into the water.

Mina continued looking upward as she sunk into the dark depths, her strange smile never leaving her porcelain face. Simon watched until he could see nothing but the crescent moon of her cheek dimly beneath the surface.

The next morning, Simon was a man obsessed. He was certain that the dream was a visitation and was reserving his strength for what he knew he would do in the evening. When Oscar knocked on his door that afternoon, he did not answer out of fear that his friend would somehow ruin his plans.

He felt reborn. Part of him felt that he had somehow lost his mind—but he was confident that by giving into Mina's request, he would be able to put himself at rest. If there were nothing to be seen in the grave but her corpse, he would resign himself to his insanity. But he had to know.

By the time the midnight hour came around, Simon found himself standing before the massive archway of Dark Hollow Cemetery, a shovel clutched tightly in his fist. Wind fluttered his long coat around his narrow body forcefully. Simon gave the graveyard a smile and let the wind rush through his teeth with a low whistle.

"I'm coming for you, Mina," he whispered, walking confidently through the gate, enjoying the feel of the cool breeze as it caressed his hair.

He stabbed the shovel into the grave joyously, sending any negative thoughts about his sanity far back into the deeper recesses of his mind. By the time he struck the wood of the coffin with the edge of the shovel, his arms were weak with exhaustion.

Simon knew that the coffin, once opened, would either send him deep into insanity, or awaken him from his madness.

The inexpensive casket opened easily and a rush of rancid air blasted into his face, the stench knocking him backwards a step. Placing his sleeve over his face, Simon leaned over the corpse.

Mina looked exquisite even in death, her white skin glowing blue by the light of the moon. Her eyes were still open, black blots on her snowy face. She was buried in a simple white dress, the folds fitting nicely to her shapely frame. Despite her beauty, Simon saw nothing that would indicate that his dream meant anything.

Mina's dress began to undulate over her stomach and a queer cry began to emit from her corpse. Removing his knife from his jacket, Simon began to carefully cut the dress away from her abdomen, tugging the fabric up so as not to cut her decaying flesh.

Pulling the folds of the dress aside, Simon stopped breathing.

A baby's face could be seen protruding from the stabbed skin of Mina's stomach. Though its eyes were closed, its mouth was moving back and forth. Tiny fingers jutted from a knife wound below its head, wiggling like worms from the loose skin. The baby cried out, its mouth wailing hollowly from the rotting stomach.

Nearly weeping, Simon began to cut carefully into Mina's flesh with the knife. Rank air erupted into his face as he sliced through the skin. Gagging, he managed to pull the baby from the stomach with a wet ripping sound, a sound not unlike removing an object from thick mud. Beetles and centipedes crawled around the warm baby like a protective shield, and Simon brushed them away.

He held the baby to his chest for a few moments, feeling its heartbeat reverberating into his bones, and placed it on the ground before a tombstone. It writhed around like a spider, but did not cry again. Though he was nearly dead with fatigue, Simon managed to cover the coffin back up with dirt.

By the time he exited the archway of Dark Hollow Cemetery, the infant held to his chest, the sun was rising on his back.

When he arrived home, Simon placed the baby in the wash basin, carefully scrubbing away the filth and insects from its pink flesh. The baby was female and he promptly named her Mina. Somehow he knew that his seed had helped create this infant, and that idea excited him on multiple levels.

The infant studied him with her hypnotic eyes—touching his soul, drawing him in with mesmerizing ease. They were Mina's eyes—he had looked into them enough times to be certain of that.

Every time he touched her she would seize his hand with her diminutive fingers, a whispery hissing trailing from her lips. "Simon," she would say, which sounded to his ears like "Sy... mon"—both slow and phonetic. Wispy dark hair stuck out of her smooth skull, her wide eyes dissecting him with unnatural wisdom.

When Oscar knocked on his door later that night, Simon let him in happily. Some part of his tired brain needed to know that what he was seeing was not merely a delirious hallucination.

"I do not like that look, my friend," Oscar said, removing his hat from his head and placing it on the table before the door. "You have the guilty face of one who has committed a very shameful sin." He grinned. "I should know. I see that face every morning as I shave. I hope I am wrong. I came by yesterday, but you did not answer the door. And I know you were lurking about."

"Hello, Oscar," Simon said, leading him into the bedroom. "I have something to show you."

Oscar smirked, his dimples shadowy blotches in the murky lighting. "You know, I'm a bit nervous as to what you are going to show me."

"You should be," Simon whispered. "I'm still not sure what it is myself."

When they entered the bedroom, Oscar gasped, his blue eyes widening as he leaned over the infant. "Dear Lord, Simon! Where did you get this little urchin?"

Simon smiled, relieved that the infant was actually there, and walked over to stand beside his friend. Mina stared at Oscar, her dark eyes sparkling with mischief.

"Do you really want to know?" Simon asked.

Oscar turned to look at his friend. "Did you kidnap her?"

"No. It's decidedly more bizarre than that. I got her from Mina's coffin. Took her right from the rotting stomach of her corpse."

"My God…" Oscar moved backwards slightly. "You've lost your mind. You're mad, Simon. You need to tell me where you got this child. We need to return her to her parents, they are probably worried sick."

Mina started to giggle, a rich and throaty sound nothing like that of an adult. "Yooo…arrrr…maaad…Sy…mon," She mimicked, erupting once again into laughter before she began to chant Oscar's words like a grotesque, sing-song nursery rhyme.

Oscar looked ill. "What in God's name is that thing?"

Simon's voice was steady, without emotion. "I don't know. You have no idea how terrified I am."

A few hours later Oscar left, promising to return with a hefty supply of brandy the next morning. By the evening, Mina was already crawling around. Simon felt his hold on reality dripping away, but he let it go. He was happy he had Mina back.

"I love you, Simon," Mina said, drool dribbling down her chin.

"I love you, too, Mina," Simon whispered, wiping away her saliva lovingly with his handkerchief.

Several months went by and, although Mina aged at the normal pace of an infant, her speech improved considerably. Oscar stopped visiting his friend as he was a little too disturbed by the strange baby. Watching an adult voice boom out of the tiny, wet lips of an infant had troubled him so profoundly that all he was able to do was stand there and shiver.

Simon killed Mina's murderer, a young doctor by the name of Ryan Harker. He broke into Harker's residence; the baby clutched protectively in his arm, and crept into the bedroom. The last thing that Harker saw as the blood spurted from his torn throat was a wide-eyed infant standing in the candlelight, an eerie grin illuminating her chubby face.

That night, Simon stood over her crib. "I did it for you, my love."

"I know, Simon," Mina whispered, her tiny fingers curling around his thumb. "Now we can live our life in peace. Someday I will be back at the point that I was when you lost me."

Simon gently shook her finger. "I know, Mina. And I will wait for you patiently. I will never leave your side. I will take care of you. I would wait forever if need be."

Many of the townspeople found the couple strangely disturbing. One look into the baby's eyes and they would practically back up and flee. There was something too disconcerting in her gaze—something too infiltrating. Simon was often spotted around town and in the local park, pushing the black, veil-covered stroller around, conversing with the baby like she was his adult companion—sometimes laughing as they argued playfully.

Even years later, when Mina was about ten, townsfolk found the father and daughter frightening. They were convinced that the couple was up to unspeakable acts of evil. Simon and Mina kept to themselves and did not often mingle with any of their neighbors.

Simon waited patiently for Mina to grow older, his love strengthening with each year. He awaited a better world, a life with a woman he had once lost.

As he walked down the rain-soaked cobbled street, Mina's pint-size warm hand clutched firmly to his own, he smiled. He felt the stares of the townspeople stab into them as they walked, but he said nothing, only smiling enigmatically. He knew that they could never have what he had.

A love that would return from the dead to be reunited with her soul mate was a rare one, and Simon knew that. He didn't mind the wait. Time was meaningless when you loved someone.

A MOMENTARY THING

Ben was studying the back of her neck, fantasizing about caressing her smooth skin, when the elevator stopped abruptly between the seventh and sixth floor. The feeling of déjà vu was incredible, but he shrugged it off, realizing that he went to work at this time every morning.

For a moment they froze, both of them waiting uncomfortably for the elevator to continue on its way.

She sighed and turned to face him, smiling sheepishly. "Let's pray that this is only a momentary thing."

Ben nodded, returning her smile, feeling himself practically melt before her gaze until she turned back to face the door. To be trapped in an elevator with a woman as beautiful as the one before him would hardly be a chore. He studied her face from the side as she kept her eyes glued to the numbers just above the elevator door. Her blonde hair was cut short in a style that emphasized her long, aristocratic nose and high cheekbones dramatically.

They waited in silence for almost a minute, but the elevator did not move. She laughed when she caught him studying her, stepped to the side unconsciously and began pushing her delicate finger onto the number seven repetitively.

He couldn't help but smile at her nervousness. The thought that she even found him remotely frightening was very amusing. Thin, bespectacled office drones like Ben did not often elicit fear in women—in fact he was usually invisible to women like the one who stood so close to him he could smell her flowery perfume.

She looked at him nervously and offered a fake smile, her

index finger still hitting the numbered button. "I can't believe this. I'm already late for the job appointment."

Ben leaned back against the wall. "If we actually get stuck here for a long time, I will vouch for you if you need it. I work in this building. It's not like it's your fault."

She seemed to relax slightly once she heard his decidedly soft-spoken voice. "Well, hopefully it won't come to that." She finally stopped pressing the button. "Besides, how long could it take to fix a damn elevator." She held her hand out shyly. "My name is Wynter. Spelled with a 'Y'."

Ben took her hand; it felt warm and soft. "That's an absolutely beautiful name. I'm the mundanely named Ben."

She laughed slightly at his joke and let go of his hand. "Ben is a fine name. It just so happens to be my father's."

They both looked up at the numbers, shifting about in the uncomfortable silence. It was as if neither of them wanted to cross a line into friendlier territory just in case the elevator started up again. A minute later, and they still had not moved.

Wynter groaned and moved toward the back of the elevator car, resting her back against the wall. "It's kind of funny really, I've always had a fear of elevators. Maybe I have a bit of psychic in me."

Ben sat down to the side, being careful not to violate her space in the small area. "Well it hasn't turned into a disastrous experience yet, has it?" He grinned and rubbed his eyes underneath his wire-rimmed glasses. "What's to be scared of anyway? Are you claustrophobic?"

Wynter nodded. "A little. My fear isn't being trapped in one though. I always had this irrational fear that the elevator cable would snap and send me plummeting several floors to my death."

"What a lovely thought," Ben said wryly. "Thanks so much for that image. Appreciate it so much."

Wynter laughed throatily, a sound that sounded so heavenly that Ben felt that she was an angel. He was not used to making women laugh—usually they just looked at him in the uneasy silence that often followed his wry observations. Dry humor was often misinterpreted as either arrogance or ignorance.

She instantly seemed to relax as she offered him an easy smirk. "I'm sorry for laughing at you. It's just that you said that so deadpan, I couldn't help it."

Ben found himself wishing he could spend the rest of his life with her. She had a certain twinkle in her eyes that he had never seen. "It was supposed to be funny."

The elevator started up suddenly; lurching itself forward as it continued its stalled ascent. Ben felt so disappointed that he thought he would weep. She had just been warming up to him, and now he would probably never see her again.

"Thank god!" she exclaimed and moved toward the door. She turned to face him. "Thanks, Ben, for taking away my discomfort with such charming ease."

Ben swallowed heavily and struggled to give himself the courage he needed to speak. "Listen. Are you doing anything this Friday?"

Just as he finished the sentence, the doors to the elevator opened. At first he mistook her expression of horror as being caused by his question, but he followed her gaze slowly to the opened doors.

About twenty feet away, a wiry, nude man stood calmly in a room full of carnage and blood puddles, a large machete-like knife clutched in his fist. Dozens of mutilated bodies were scattered around him, some of them so butchered it was nearly impossible to tell if they were human. Although his shaved head remained toward the ground, his eyes moved up slowly until they locked onto the open doors of the elevator. A slow, menacing smile lit up under his blood-splattered face like the skin blistering flame of a blowtorch. He began to swing the machete like a pendulum—the smile widening as he began to rock his head to the side casually like a snake. He began to whistle through his teeth softly at first, but within seconds it rose to an ear-shattering peak.

Ben was already slamming his fingers into the buttons as the man began to walk slowly toward them. The man broke out into a run, wailing shrilly as he ran.

The doors closed just as the blade of the machete came down between them. Ben watched the blood drenched blade rise to the ceiling in morbid fascination as they descended.

Ben and Wynter looked at each other, their pale faces devoid of all color in the sickly fluorescent lighting. The elevator continued to descend toward the first floor as they tried to think of something to say. The only sound was their labored and anxious breathing.

The elevator came to a halt on the bottom floor and the doors opened up slowly. Both of them waited momentarily, listening to the silence as if it held insidious secrets.

Standing in the lobby were Ben and Wynter, or exact duplicates of them, their entire bodies drenched with blood. The doubles stared at them silently, their eyes studying them fearfully. Their hair stood out at crazy angles, the blood providing a perverse kind of hair gel.

"Oh my god," Ben's blood drenched double said, staring toward the elevator door in horror.

"What the hell is going on?" Ben whispered, not wishing to leave the security of the elevator. "That's...us."

"Please wake me," Wynter said, her voice quivering.

While they stood there in uncertainty, the metal doors softly closed, and the elevator began to ascend again.

"Oh fuck," Ben hissed fearfully and launched his finger at the number pad. The car gently came to a stop and the doors slid open quietly.

The figure that stood before them had the appearance of a surreal, drug induced nightmare. He wore a wide brimmed hat, which rose up and down on his head like a toy sailboat above his closed, vein covered eyelids. A long, black trench coat undulated over his flesh, pulsating up and down around his obese body. His crimson cheeks were plump, almost as if he had stuffed a rag into his mouth. Thin, insect legs protruded painfully from his face, twitching around spasmodically as if they were struggling to explode from his flesh. Eight, hairy spider legs protruded over his upper lip like a living mustache, writhing slowly as they tickled at his mouth. He moved his fingers in snake like motions, almost as if he was playing a phantom piano and smiled widely, sending dozens of tiny spiders scurrying from his mouth.

The man's eyes fluttered open, sounding not unlike the flickering of an insect's wings and he stared at them with dimly lit green eyes. He studied them quietly for a moment; almost seeming to feed off of their silent fear like it was electrical. Ben and Wynter stood rigidly, their bodies still—perhaps feeling that movement would bring the man upon them.

Then, almost as if he found their fear amusing, he began to titter softly, his giggling escaping his lips alongside dozens of insects. The laughter increased rapidly, his corpulent body vibrating with every wave of glee. As he laughed, the flesh on his face began to rip apart softly, sending an army of spiders pouring from his torn face and onto the floor.

Ben began to jam his finger onto the number pad as Wynter retreated to the back of the elevator, shrieking so loudly that the noise cut into his eardrums like little tiny razor blades of sound. She put her back to the wall and began to kick at some of the scurrying spiders hysterically.

The man pulled his coat open, revealing his obscenely, massive stomach. Thousands of insect legs stuck out of his waving flesh like hair. As he continued to laugh, his body ruptured in a detonation of insects and flesh, sending a wave of them into the elevator car just before the doors closed. Rancid air filled the car like a physical presence, blasting into their nostrils like dirty, corrupting fingers.

They descended to the next floor, both of them shrieking in disgust as the hundreds of insects scrambled about their feet. A fat spider with black and yellow legs bit Ben's forearm and he slapped it away with repulsion.

Ben pushed the emergency stop button and tried to get himself under control. Within minutes, he and Wynter had been able to stomp out most of the insects and now the hard floor was slippery with the remains. Ben felt his legs shaking underneath his weight in little tremors of fear. Winter was sobbing in the corner, her eyes never leaving the door. After a minute, they managed to get themselves under some form of control.

They stood in front of the numbered display and studied it like a book.

Although Ben felt like weeping and sweat was burning into

his eyes, he managed to chase the panic back down his throat. Wynter was rocking back and forth tensely, her eyes darting around the elevator for signs of movement. He could tell that she was about to give in once again to the panic and he certainly wouldn't blame her, he was dangerously close to shrieking himself.

Ben sighed. "I think the best thing for us to remain sane is to take everything in stride and not think about how fantastic it is. It's happening to us, and we need to accept it. That fucker upstairs looked real enough to me."

Wynter nodded. "Okay, but if we get out of this, I'm going to scream and cry like a little girl."

He smiled. "Me too. Now, let's find a floor that might be a little safer."

"Any preferences?"

Ben shook his head. "You pick it. I picked the last one and look where that left us."

Wynter took Ben's hand in her own and pushed the number eight, squeezing tightly as the elevator began to move upward. They held their breaths simultaneously as the car came to a halt.

The doors opened up leisurely, revealing a brightly-lit hallway. The floors, walls and ceiling were white and although the room was brilliantly lit, there was no discernible light source.

Ben narrowed his eyes and studied the hallway for signs of danger. "I don't like the way this feels."

Wynter pulled his arm slightly and led him from the car. "You work in this building, don't you? Ever seen this hallway before?"

"I've worked in this building for five years and, no, I've never seen this hallway." He grinned and squeezed her damp hand. "Can't say I've ever had the pleasure of working with Spidey down there either, though."

She laughed nervously. "Stop. Don't make me laugh. Doing that now makes me feel like I'm laughing at a funeral." She ran her hand over the smooth, clinically clean surface of the wall. "This place looks like the set of a Stanley Kubrick film."

Ben sighed. "Oh, that's got to be a great omen."

They walked cautiously, their bodies ready to flee at the first signs of movement.

"By the way, yes," Wynter whispered as they moved down the hallway.

They were now about thirty feet from the safety of the elevator.

He looked at her in confusion. "Yes, what?"

"We wake up from this nightmare alive and, yes, I'll go out with you this Friday." She smiled radiantly, her cheekbones rising up.

"But only if we get out of this alive," Ben said dryly. "If I die, the date is off."

They turned the corner only to find it was a dead end.

Wynter was running her hands over the smooth surface of the wall, feeling to see if they were missing something, when a hot bead of moisture hit the top of her hand. It was a blood droplet.

Ben saw it too, as more blood began to come from the surface of the wall. The red droplets stood out shockingly on the snowy surface. A faint roar was emanating from the wall and they looked into each other's eyes, feeling the panic enter their bodies as if through osmosis.

Plaster began to fall to the floor as the building shook underneath them. The blood began to splash their shoes as the floor began to tremble, sending faint vibrations into their bodies. They both turned to flee in the other direction, their panic stricken eyes wide with alarm.

The wall detonated in a crimson explosion, blood erupting into the hallway. Ben risked one look back before they slid around the corner and saw that they would drown long before they could escape.

The crimson wall blasted into them, sending them down the hallway at a frightening speed. They sailed through the open doors of the elevator and slammed into the wall violently. Within seconds, they were underneath the surface, their mouths filling with the thick, iron taste of the blood.

Frantically, Ben searched through the dark liquid for the numbered buttons. He swam forward and belted his hand into the first surface he felt. His hand collided with the keypad and he jammed his fingers into the buttons.

The elevator began to move downwards, sending them floating to the ceiling, the pressure holding them to the top of the car as they descended. Ben screamed, sending a rush of hot blood down his throat. He felt Wynter grasp his arm tightly as they floated, their bodies held fast to the surface.

When the doors opened, they found themselves hurling from the emptying elevator, spinning around in the liquid as they went.

Coughing and sputtering weakly, they looked up to see dozens of office workers standing around them in the thick, red puddles. Ben wiped the blood from his eyes and stood up quickly, still feeling the effects of the adrenaline rush he had experienced.

He helped Wynter to her feet and couldn't help but thinking that the blood made her look like the wounded survivor of a horror movie. Every part of her body was drenched in red, only her wide eyes stood out against the scarlet liquid.

"Ben, what the hell are you doing?" John Reynolds said. Reynolds was his boss.

"We're back?" Ben asked, studying his boss as if there was a lit fuse on his head, backing up slowly as he spoke. He did not trust reality at the moment.

Reynolds looked confused. "What the hell are you talking about? You don't just come walking into this office after being gone for a year and say 'we're back'. It doesn't work like that in the real world, Ben. Everybody was worried sick about you."

Ben laughed bitterly. "Do I look like I just came waltzing in? We're covered in fucking blood for Christ's sake."

The other workers stood around uncomfortably, looking away every time Ben would meet their gaze. Wynter grabbed his hand and held it tightly.

"Ben, have you gone insane?" Reynolds asked. "I don't see any blood. I think you better get back on that elevator and leave the building."

Ben and Wynter turned to look at each other and immediately broke out into laughter, despite the fact the blood was congealing on their clothes and hair. The crowd just stood around uneasily and watched them like animals at a zoo. None of them realized they were standing around in puddles of hardening blood.

"No thanks, John," Ben said, as they walked away. "We'll take the stairs."

When they arrived at the final flight, they stopped.

When they reached the lobby, everything was unnaturally still. It was empty, which was unusual for any time of the day. Even at night, there would be a security guard.

They heard a soft clicking sound and looked behind them at the dreaded elevator. The light was lit up on seven and the light slowly began to descend toward the lower numbers.

They stood rigid and watched the numbers count down gradually like the ticking of a bomb.

When the car reached the final number, there was a soft bell and the doors slid easily open. Inside the elevator were the doubles of Ben and Wynter, their mouths dropping down simultaneously in a moment that would almost had been comic had been not been so terrified.

"Oh my god," Ben said, staring toward the elevator door in awe. Seeing a perfect replica of himself was even more unnerving than seeing the horrific monster he had seen on the floor above.

"What the hell is going on?" Ben's double whispered, staring out from the open door of the elevator with wide eyes. "That's… us."

"Please wake me," Wynter's double said.

The doors closed and the numbered lights began to count as the elevator ascended yet again. Ben and Wynter stood in the lobby of the building, their bodies stiff as their brains tried to comprehend what they just saw.

Ben was the first to speak. "If that's us, they—we are in for a big surprise when they get to the next floor."

Ben walked over to elevator door and studied the numbers. Although every core of his body screamed for him to flee, he found himself pushing the call number of the elevator.

"Ben, what the fuck are you doing?" Wynter whispered. "Why did you just bring the elevator back down? Let's get the hell out of here."

Ben shook his head. "Do you honestly feel that it's safe to go outside? Don't you notice that there is nothing out there? No cars or people? Pretty odd for Manhattan, don't you think?"

Wynter looked toward the revolving doors and saw that he was right. The normally crowded streets were silent.

Ben's eyes never left the lighted numbers. He stood unbending as the numbers began to count back down to the lobby, his body tensing. Every time a number lit up, it was followed by a soft click.

They held their breaths as the last number lit up. The doors slid open, once again shocking them ever closer to insanity.

Two corpses lay sprawled in the elevator car.

Although Ben could only see the back of his head, he knew it was his own. His right arm hung off grotesquely, nearly severed off. It still spurted blood, indicating that he had just been killed. Wynter's body was against the wall, half of her head missing. Her one eye was still filled with the terror of what she had last glimpsed and her arm twitched spasmodically, a residue of still firing nerves.

Ben began to giggle insanely, his mind shattering like little fragments of glass. He turned to face Wynter, tiny spasms of laughter still erupting from his throat. "Going up, my dear?"

"Are you deranged?" Wynter said, moving forward to grab his arm. "Get the hell out of there."

"Actually, I didn't think so until I saw that," Ben said, his eyes moving past her.

Wynter followed his gaze and felt a feeling of panic detonate in her chest like a hand grenade.

The man who stood only seven feet away from her was completely hairless. His spacious eyes were black, with no eyelids, which gave him a reptilian, unblinking look. His skin was an unnatural, deathly white. Black veins snaked all around his bald, pale white head, looking almost like tattoos. He wore some kind of dark military uniform, which covered him up completely, making his white head and hands stand out in stark contrast. He grinned broadly, exposing square shaped, metallic teeth. Flames licked through the cracks in his teeth like fiery serpents in a crematorium. The man cocked his head to the side like a predator.

Wynter rushed into the car, screaming when she saw her

own mutilated body against the elevator wall. Ben pushed a random number grimly, and watched the doors close like the incoming blade of a guillotine. As the elevator began to ascend, he felt his nervousness suddenly break away like a depleted storm, his energy exhausted. He closed his eyes as they rose and listened peacefully to the sound of Wynter's weeping. Her cries accompanied the elevator music, a classical piece by Gregor Handel, like a perverted symphony.

"Look on the bright side," he whispered calmly, his eyes still closed as he waited for the doors to open. "We're not really going to die. We're probably doomed to repeat this over and over for eternity." He smiled, inhaling deeply of the stale, blood scented air. "In fact, I bet we're down in the lobby right now, waiting for the elevator to come back down."

The doors of the elevator opened, and a wave of hot air rushed into his face. His eyes were still closed when the blade of the machete nearly severed his arm, slicing into his bone painfully. The last sound that he heard before he fell into unconsciousness was Wynter's shrill scream.

Ben was studying the back of her neck, fantasizing about caressing her smooth skin, when the elevator stopped abruptly between the seventh and sixth floor. The feeling of déjà vu was incredible, but he shrugged it off, realizing that he went to work at this time every morning.

For a moment, they froze, both of them waiting uncomfortably for the elevator to continue on its way.

She sighed and turned to face him, smiling sheepishly. "Let's pray that this is only a momentary thing."

EXCEPT FOR OPHELIA

CARVERTON: VICTORIAN ERA

The naked corpse of a young woman lay in the center of the forest clearing, dark shadows twisting around her smooth face as an icy breeze swayed the branches. A full moon, surrounded by shimmering stars, shone beyond the clearing, illuminating the landscape in a murky glow.

A man stood before the body, head low, his long trench coat billowing softly in the wind like a whisper. A bloody dagger dropped from his hand and into the dew-drenched grass. He removed the wide brimmed hat from his head and let his long black hair fall onto his shoulders. A long aristocratic nose made his snow-white face look regal. Clutching the hat to his chest, he stared at the moon and began to sing a lullaby, his voice so low it would have sounded like nothing more than a hiss had there not been such a beautiful melody.

The corpse was wrenched to its feet as if by spectral puppet strings, its arms and legs jerking awkwardly about. Her blood-caked hair protruded out in stick-like strands. Blood ran from the stab marks in her chest and down onto her thighs as she was pulled around, hands waving spastically. The man continued to croon, his voice rising into a falsetto, his left hand flickering around as if he were conducting an orchestra.

"Ian, must you play such foolish games?" A woman's voice asked from behind one of the trees.

Ian stopped singing, and the corpse fell to the ground in a macabre tangle of arms and legs. He turned to face the woman as she entered the clearing from the forest. "Ophelia, must you always intrude?"

The woman was entirely in white, black hair lay across her back in silky strands. She walked toward the corpse, her hips swinging seductively underneath her flowing dress. Turning to face her stepson, she smiled, her cheekbones giving her face a predatory appearance. Dark bangs hung onto her porcelain forehead, her flesh moonlight-blue. Her eyes sparkled as she stared at Ian.

"This one is beautiful," Ophelia purred, staring down at the corpse before planting a kiss on Ian's cheek. "Where did you find her?"

"The town is having the yearly carnival. She is the daughter of one of the gypsies."

"You are such a charmer, Ian," Ophelia said. "Just like your father. But you have much to learn about reanimation. You were making her dance like a broken puppet." She let her penetrating gaze turn back toward the corpse. "Death makes her so much more beautiful."

Ian smiled, placing the black hat back upon his head. "Ah, but how would you know, my dear? You did not even see her when she was alive."

"Death always brings out the beauty in a woman," Ophelia said, twirling a black curl in her finger mischievously.

Ian pulled the curl away from her hand. "I think you should leave me be. I want to practice the dance some more."

"Take me to the carnival, Ian. I feel like being around people tonight."

"That would not be a good idea, Ophelia. Someone may have seen me leave with this gypsy girl. It could mean trouble."

"Nonsense," she whispered, running her finger along his rigid jawbone. "No one notices a poor gypsy girl." Her full lips pulled back from her teeth in a feral grin. "Come on, Ian. We have not had a date in a long time! It will be fun!"

"We must not take another victim tonight, Ophelia," Ian said, looking at her sideways. "If we do, the woods will be crawling with hunters by morning."

"I just want to go in and soak in some of the atmosphere,"

she said, taking his hand. "Is there dancing? It has been so long since I have danced."

Ian allowed himself to be led through the dark woods, loving the way her hand felt in his. "There is a dance, my dear. But is it wise to flaunt yourself? Every man there will wish to bed you."

"It is for the better if we get attention. Would they suspect you of killing the young woman if they see you on my arm? I think not."

As they walked hand in hand through the gloomy trees, Ian marveled at the way the moonlight could be seen peeking through the branches of the stark limbs above. Living within the thick forest outside of the town of Carverton only allowed him to see patches of the nighttime sky.

On some nights, he would climb one of the taller trees until he felt as if he could touch the heavens.

The moon was mysterious and enchanting—nothing made him feel more alive. He loved the way it gave his white flesh an otherworldly bluish glow. Sometimes, as he lay comfortably in the branches far above the ground, he would reach his hand out as if he could pluck stars from the sky like glittering jewels. He always imagined if he were able to steal a star from the sky, that he would give it to the moon. No woman was as beautiful, nor could a woman instill him with the power he felt when gazing upon its radiant surface.

Except for Ophelia.

"You spend too much time longing for the sky, Ian," Ophelia whispered in his ear, her tongue flickering at his lobe like a serpent. "The real world is here down below. You should live in it once in awhile."

They entered a clearing. Ophelia's white skin looked dark blue without the trees to shield the moonlight. Ian longed to run his hands over her flesh, but feared his father would take revenge.

"Thinking the night sky beautiful is not unhealthy," Ian said, tucking his hair behind his ears. He placed his wide brimmed hat on his head. "I could never tire of looking at it."

"Do you not think I am beautiful?" she asked.

Ian took her hand to his red lips, bowed down, and kissed her smooth flesh. "I have always thought you beautiful, Ophelia. Perhaps the most beautiful creature I have ever known. I adore you."

"Then why do you not try to take advantage of me?"

"Because I fear my father. As should you."

"Dante has been gone for ten years. He is most likely dead. How long could he last outside the safety of the forest, Ian? There are not many places left for our kind. The world is changing. The old days are dead and gone. We can no longer mingle as easily."

"Dead he *may* be…but I, for one, am not taking the chance. He would crucify me for bedding his love."

"I have bedded hundreds of men since he vanished."

Ian grinned crookedly, cheekbones rising on his dark face. "And how many of those men are alive?"

"You are too much like your father, Ian. Too clever and delicious for your own good. Those men died because they could not handle me. Dante did not kill even one of those men." She stopped, pulling him to her fiercely, removing his hat. His hair fell around his ears.

Ian watched her calmly, feeling her warm breath rush into his face. It smelled of flowers. "You are in quite a mood tonight, Ophelia," he whispered.

She moved closer, her wet lips brushing over his. "Give me one night, Ian. Even if your father is alive, there is no way he could know." She turned his head and nibbled on his ear. "The moon has only been in the sky for an hour. We can spend a little time here in this clearing and then enjoy the rest of the evening at the carnival. It always lasts until dawn."

Ian inhaled her breath deeply, eyes closed. "I cannot do this, Ophelia. I fear my father far too much."

Ophelia smiled widely, her perfect white teeth gleaming in the moonlight. "I'll never give up."

Ian took her hand back in his, leading her back through the woods. "I would not want you to."

They spoke very little as they walked through the dense trees that bordered the town of Carverton. It wasn't long until they began to hear the music of the carnival, a dim roar of laughter and clapping, accompanied by a few instruments. The smell of roasted lamb and freshly baked bread was heavy in the forest air. Up ahead in the distance, they saw the inviting flickering of torch light at the edge of the trees.

"Please do not make a scene," Ian said just as they walked into the warm light.

Ophelia pulled his arm tighter and grinned like a child. "Worry not, young Ian. I shall only be myself."

"That is what I am worried about."

The carnival could best be described as an elegant chaos. A storyteller sat at the edge of the trees, strumming a small guitar before a group of enraptured children, their cherubic faces glowing in the campfire. Various fortuneteller wagons surrounded the clearing, beautiful young gypsy women standing outside to entice the townsfolk. Dozens of food tents dotted the area, the heady smells mixing together enticingly. A half naked snake charmer watched his serpent sway back and forth with a mysterious smile, his fingers gliding gently over his flute. Ian noticed the father of the woman he had killed looking around at the various patrons nervously for a sign of his missing daughter.

On the far side of the clearing was a small band, consisting of a few violinists, a lute player, clad entirely in red, and an African drummer, who had completely surrounded himself with his instruments. A few of the young men and women of the town danced quietly before the musicians.

Ophelia sauntered toward the band, swaying to the seductive beat.

Ian followed her through the crowd, ignoring the stares of the younger women as he walked. One victim from the carnival was definitely enough.

Ophelia stepped into the circle of people as Ian caught up. She spun gracefully, her dark hair flowing about her head as if she had stepped out of a celestial daydream. She was smiling as if she had just put a piece of heavenly chocolate on her tongue, head held back as if she was about to moan. She pulled the folds of her dress around her as she danced, giving her audience a tantalizing peek of her muscled thighs.

Many of the men gathered around to watch, ignoring the heated looks from their own wives and lovers. Even the snake charmer, his serpent coiled about his arm, walked up to watch Ophelia.

Ophelia locked eyes with Ian as she danced, enjoying the lustful way he stared at her. Much to Ian's annoyance, she pulled the cobra from the snake charmer's grasp, holding it before her face until she could feel the flickering of its tongue upon her dark lips. She spun around the circle, the serpent wrapped around her arm.

In a movement so quick it was but a blur, the snake lunged forward and bit Ophelia in the neck. Two thin streams of blood dripped from the fang holes.

The music stopped and the crowd stared at Ophelia, eyes wide.

Ophelia dropped the cobra to her feet and touched her neck, staring at the blood on her fingertips. Then she gave them a slow smile, her dark eyes flashing dangerously in the torchlight, and put her bloody fingers to her lips.

"Witch!" one of the gypsy women shrieked.

There was silence in the clearing, Ophelia staring down the members of the crowd one by one with her confident gaze.

"I can assure you, I am certainly not a witch," Ophelia said, offering a bloody grin.

A gypsy man with a full head of dark curly hair launched himself forward, grabbing Ophelia's left arm. "Whatever you are, woman! You will burn just as easily!"

Ophelia growled and raked her fingers across the man's throat, splashing her white face and dress with crimson droplets. The man fell to the ground, clutching at his neck as he choked, blood gushing out into the green grass. Ophelia held her splattered head high, staring defiantly at the shocked crowd.

Two more men, one of them carrying a large dagger, threw themselves at Ophelia, taking her down to the grass. The crowd fled the clearing, screaming as they ran, knocking over stands of food and merchandise.

Ian leapt to her aid, pulling one of the men away and

snapping his neck with a quick flash of his hands.

Ophelia tore away a piece of the man's flesh with her teeth, eyes glowing yellow by the torchlight.

Everyone had fled the clearing, leaving Ophelia and Ian standing over the bloodied corpses of the men they had slain. Ian was breathing hard, eyes darting around the carnival for any further attacks.

"We better get back into the forest," Ian said, turning to face his stepmother.

"I won't be able to go far," Ophelia said, nodding at her leg. A massive knife wound was on her calf, the exposed flesh glistening in the torchlight.

Ian shook his head and grabbed her hand. "You dug your own grave, Ophelia. You did not have to play with the serpent." He picked her up and threw her over his shoulder. "We cannot move very fast like this."

The sounds of dogs barking penetrated the still air, followed by the deep yells of some of the men.

Ian frowned and moved away from the carnival and into the shadows. "The cemetery is just over here. Perhaps we can use the dead to mask our scents."

Thick fog seeped into their surroundings from the nearby lake, and Ian welcomed it, hoping it would hide them. They came to the stone wall that surrounded the front of the graveyard and followed it to the arched entranceway. Ian thought briefly about entering the boarded up church that resided just in front of the graveyard, but decided it would be much too easy to be trapped inside. With a quick glance at the twin angel statues that guarded the stone archway, Ian entered Dark Hollow Cemetery, letting the darkness engulf them.

Ian stopped about one hundred yards inside and placed Ophelia onto one of the larger tombstones. She was giggling, despite the fact that the barking, and shouts of the men were moving closer.

"I am happy that you can find humor in all of this, Ophelia," Ian said. "It was a mistake to come in here. We will not be able to get out now. We are trapped inside."

Off near the entrance to the graveyard, they could see the

flickering of more than a dozen torches.

They stood in front of a mausoleum that had the name *'Anna Wilde'* stenciled on the front. Underneath her name were letters that looked like they had recently been written—*'Nathan Wilde'*.

In the front of the crypt, a little off to the right, was a massive oak tree. The branches drew crooked black lines as they snaked over the chalky surface of the luminous moon above. The moonlight lit up the landscape around them much more brightly than Ian was comfortable with. The humans, even with their rather weak eyes, would be able to see them if they moved too much. Some of the gravestones were so bright that they glowed.

Ophelia sat back against a tombstone with a pained grimace and looked toward the entrance. "I do not think they will come in. I just heard one of them ranting about the devil. They think we are demons. They will most likely wait until the morning."

Ian frowned. "And then what, Ophelia? They will kill us easily in large numbers. We need to get out of here *now*. And you do not know that they will wait until morning. They could come in here within minutes."

"The gate is much too high for you to carry me out. It looks to me that you may have to leave me behind, Ian. I am not used to seeing your handsome face in this bright of a light. You look so much like your father it is chilling."

Ian grabbed his stepmother by the wrist. "Do you ever stop? We are about to be killed. This is *very* serious."

"I have been alive for a long time, Ian. It is difficult to be serious about life when you are as old as I am. It does not look good for me. Stay with me until they storm through the gate and then climb over the wall. The back entrance has a iron fence, but it is still much too high for me to cross."

"I will not do that, Ophelia. I will stay with you even if it means my death. I killed by your side at the carnival. I killed that woman in the woods. I will face the repercussions with you."

"Do not be a fool, Ian. You are still but a youth." She looked around at the glowing tombstones and nodded. "It is as you said, I have quite literally dug my own grave."

Ian shook his head. "We will find a way."

Ophelia ran her hands over a tombstone, brushing away dead leaves. "I have always loved cemeteries. They have a serene elegance. There is a quiet beauty about the way the dead keep their secrets. Where do you think they go once they cross over to the other side?"

Ian did not take his eyes away from the torchlight. "I do not have a clue. There are spirits in this cemetery, so I know they go somewhere."

"Spirits?" Ophelia asked, looking around the graveyard curiously. "I've never seen one. How do you know there are spirits?"

Ian looked away from the entrance and pointed to the starry sky, placing his index finger in the center of the skull-white moon. "One night while I was laying in the branches watching the stars, I saw two spirits."

"You are jesting."

"I really did, Ophelia. It was two of them. They looked human, but opaque. I could see the stars within their bodies. It looked as if they were made of glass. They danced by, twirling around above the trees. It was so exquisite. I heard the woman laugh. They flew toward the cemetery."

"Why did you never tell me this before, Ian? That is beautiful."

"I did not think you would believe me."

"I am not sure I do believe you."

"I would never lie to you."

Ophelia's ravishing smile grew mischievous. "Never?"

Ian shook his head and looked back toward the gate. "Never. What would be the point?"

"Do you lust after me?"

Ian chuckled. "You never stop do you? Ophelia, we are in real danger here. We could be killed."

"Do not stray from the question, Ian. You said you would never lie to me. Do you lust for me?"

"Yes. I always have. You know this—I know you do. It is why you never leave me alone. You are absolutely unremitting! Even when father was around you drove me mad—a glance here, a flash of your breast there, a touch of your hand! Absolutely mad! I find you exquisite. I hate my father for finding you first and I despise him for leaving you. I think about you all the time—especially when you disappear for months." He stopped, his face registering that he felt he had said too much. "Why can you not just leave me in peace?"

Ophelia's eyes twinkled. "It feels good to hear you speak of me in such a way." She leaned over and kissed him on the cheek. "I love you, Ian."

Ian stared into her eyes for a few seconds before kissing her back on the lips. He smelled lilac on her breath and he exhaled as he brushed his tongue into hers, taking her air into his lungs.

"I love you, too," Ian said, pulling away, saying each word with her own sweet breath.

Ophelia put her hand on his cheek. "You only did that because you do not think we are going to make it out of here alive."

"Very, very true," Ian said, letting his gaze turn back toward the growing number of torches.

"You are going to regret the kiss—and your words if we escape."

"Yes I will both completely. It is doubtful we will get out."

"I have a way to get us out," Ophelia said, standing up and facing the mausoleum.

Ian turned to face her. "Don't play games, Ophelia. If you have a way, tell me now."

She pointed at the mausoleum and the wind fluttered at her blood splattered sleeve. "Anna and Nathan Wilde will help us." She turned back at him and grinned. Ian had never seen her more beautiful. "It is a good thing you have been practicing your reanimation."

Ian nodded. "This could work."

"It *will* work," Ophelia said, walking up the stone steps.

Ian watched her as she ascended toward the mausoleum door, marveling at the cat-like way she moved, then followed. She pushed on the door and it creaked reluctantly open, the moonlight sending a soft glow onto the stone floor within. The stench of decay immediately drifted out into the cool night.

Two coffins lay side by side in the center of the dimly lit stone room. A table rested against the far wall, a single unlit candle in the center. A wooden chair was to their right; the seat lit up in the pale light.

"The one on the right is very new," Ian said, grimacing. "The smell is unbearable."

"Good," Ophelia said. "It will make it much more effective."

Both coffins were sealed, but Ian had little trouble getting them opened. A youthful woman rested in the left coffin, or at least Ian thought she was young, her face was covered with a strange death mask. The lips, eyes, and brows were all painted in thin, sketch-like lines, giving the impression of a living doll. The smile on the mask was haunting and mysterious. In the second coffin was the body of an older man, his white bearded face appearing almost azure by the dim lighting.

Ophelia began to sing, her voice sounding otherworldly in the enclosed confines of the mausoleum. She gestured rapidly with her hands, flickering them around her face in a dizzying blur.

The melody echoed off the walls, as if there were a chorus of angels singing within the crypt. Ian raised his head and listened, enchanted by her radiant voice.

Anna Wilde jerked straight up in her coffin, head cocking to the side as though she were an animal. She brought her hand up stiffly and removed her death mask, revealing a nearly skeletal face. Pieces of her jaw and cheekbones protruded from her leathery skin.

Ian joined Ophelia, their voices melding seamlessly together.

Nathan Wilde rose up from his casket, mouth hanging slack. His eyes were hard and sunk deep into the confines of his decaying face.

The two corpses climbed clumsily down from their coffins and lurched toward the door of the mausoleum. Ian and Ophelia chanted just behind them, their hands moving in perfect sync.

The corpses exited through the doors of the mausoleum and into the moonlight, Anna's burial dress billowing softly behind as they descended the stone steps.

Ian and Ophelia guided the corpses through the cemetery,

their faces wet with perspiration. Anna and Nathan wobbled toward the torchlight, moving through the radiant tombstones as though someone from above had connected their limbs to strings. As soon as they reached the arched entrance, the men began to scream and fire their guns. Dogs barked ferociously.

Anna and Nathan took each other hand in hand and began to dance around the men crudely, unaware of the bullets that pierced their dead flesh. One of the men lit Anna's dress afire with his torch, but the corpses continued to spin around, the flames scorching their flesh black. The stench was immediate.

The men fled. Shouts of, "The undead are attacking the town!" could be heard.

Ian and Ophelia stopped singing at once, and Anna and Nathan Wilde promptly fell to the ground before the cemetery opening, their flesh still flickering with weak flames, smoke rising into the twin angels above.

Ophelia giggled, covering her mouth with her hand.

Ian took hold of her arm. "We need to leave now!"

"I will not forget what you said, Ian," Ophelia said, giving her stepson a knowing nod.

He stared into her black eyes before picking her up and carrying her toward the still burning corpses. "I do not expect you to, Ophelia."

They hastily exited the cemetery and vanished into the forest, their dark forms quickly fusing with the trees that had been the home of their kind for thousands of years.

FAMILY PLOTTING

"Do you honestly believe that?" Fred asked, staring down at the bloodied corpse. A knife protruded from her open mouth. "Do you honestly believe I had something to do with this?"

Peter stared down at the corpse. The dead blonde couldn't have been more than twenty years old. Her eyes were wide, as if she had been shrieking when the knife was thrust between her teeth. Her white neck was splattered with crimson drops.

The living room appeared as if it hadn't been cleaned in weeks. Pizza boxes and dirty laundry littered the room. The room smelled of sweat and rotting food.

Fred ran his hands through his shoulder length brown hair. "I admit I've gone off the handle before, Peter, but I swear I didn't kill this girl. I swear to fucking God, man."

Peter sighed, wishing he had never come. He knew he should not have answered the phone. "Okay, Freddy, tell me everything again. You were fucking rambling before. I don't think I understood a word."

"You're gonna get pissed at me."

"I'm already pissed at you, Fred. I don't hear from you for almost a year, my own brother. I finally hear something and you want me to help you with this?" Peter let his voice drop to a dangerous whisper. "Tell me what the hell happened. Stop playing fucking games."

"She's a prostitute. I picked her up down near Bennet Street."

Peter closed his eyes as if it pained him to think. "Do you know how fucking bad this sounds, Freddy? Do you know how guilty you look? You have a goddamn dead whore on your living room carpet with a knife sticking out of her fucking mouth."

"Are you going to let me tell my story?"

Peter growled.

Fred nodded, adjusting his red sweater around his pudgy belly. "Okay. We came back here and we drank a little. We agreed on a price and then she gave me a blowjob. I went to the bathroom for a quick shower, and when I got back out she was like this."

"Did she swallow?"

"I can't believe you want those kind of details. The poor girl is dead, man. Give her some dignity."

Peter clenched his teeth over his bottom lip as if chasing back a scream. "Listen. I didn't ask you if the whore swallowed so that I could get off on it. She's dead on your carpet, Freddy! If she swallowed your load, what the *hell* you going to do? The police will be able to get anything they want about you if your semen is swimming around in her stomach."

"Oh. No, she didn't swallow. I used a condom. I flushed it down the toilet."

"Well that's a plus. Now tell me the rest."

"There is no more. I told you everything. I called you as soon as I saw the body."

Peter stared at Fred, looking as if he was fighting the urge to pound his face, nostrils flaring widely above his well-trimmed goatee. "Freddy, how the fuck do you expect the police to buy this story? This can't be the real story."

"Peter, it's the truth, man. I swear to God it is. Do you know how much like Daddy you look right now?"

"Did you ever meet this girl before? Do you even know her name?"

"No, I never met her. I think she said her name was Angel."

Peter kicked against the girl's head and a thin stream of blood fell down the side of her face. Needle tracks dotted her arm and in between her fingers. "A whore named Angel. Heh. I doubt that's her real name. Okay, so you picked up a girl you never met. You're trying to tell me that you then went to take a shower while a fucking junkie whore was in your house?"

"It was only for like two minutes, Peter. That's it."

"I still don't buy it. No one is stupid enough to let a stranger alone in their house—especially a prostitute. "

Fred sat down on the beer stained couch. "Somebody must have came into the apartment, stabbed her and then taken off."

"Is that your knife?"

Fred looked dazed for a moment as if he did not understand the question. He leaned over the end table and took a long look at the corpse. "Yeah. That knife is from my kitchen. It's the only one I own."

"Freddy, this is getting fucking ridiculous. Admit you killed this whore and I will help you. This is the kind of thing I do for a living. I can make it better for you. I'm not going to do shit for you if you keep lying. Too goddamn dangerous."

"Peter, I told you I was telling the truth."

"Freddy, goddammit! I will walk out this fucking door and leave you with her to rot!"

"Peter, I swear to God, man!"

"Freddy...listen to me. Why the fuck would someone sneak into your house, kill a junkie whore, then leave without taking anything? It doesn't make any sense. Who would want to frame you? You have shit."

"I'm sorry, Peter."

Peter turned to his brother, studying him. Fred had gained about thirty pounds and he looked like he hadn't shaved in at least a month. His eyes were bloodshot. He looked like a typical drugbag loser, a far cry from the same younger brother who left the family to get away from all the drugs and the violence.

"I don't believe you, Freddy," Peter finally said. "You gotta stop acting so fucking stupid. If you're going to get a blowjob from a whore, just get one in your car—don't be taking them home and letting them see where you live. That shit could be dangerous. You're my kid brother. I want you to stay safe."

"I know it was stupid. I've been so lonely, Peter. You have no idea how much. I just can't seem to make nothing work anymore. My luck is shit. Tonight was only a prime example of that. The reason I took a shower while she was there was because we talked a little bit. I was kind of hoping she'd stick around and maybe talk."

Peter grimaced. "I realize you're lonely, Fred—I can see it on your face. But I gotta tell ya, man. Trying to strike up a loving friendship with junkie whores ain't gonna get you nowhere. Besides, what the hell you going to talk about? Sucking dick? Or where to get the best heroin? Please. They don't care about nothing except their next high. They'll do anything to get it."

Fred offered a painful smile. "Damn right. Like give oral sex to the likes of me. Do you know how pathetic I feel trying to romance a prostitute? I feel lower than low, man."

"I didn't say that, Freddy. It's like you said. It's just a run of bad luck. Things have a way of changing quick. I always thought that you would be the one to turn out good once you got away from the family." He stared down at the corpse. "And I know you can do better than this. Hell, I could have set you up with a dozen whores better than this tired young thing."

Fred pointed at his pockmarked face. "Not with this mug. I've only slept with two women who I didn't have to pay to have sex with me."

"Sometimes it's not about how you look, but how you carry yourself. You need some confidence."

"I wish I had it, Peter. Daddy fucked me up bad."

Peter sighed at the mention of his father. "Daddy brought you up the other day when we were talking about old times. Said he wished you would have joined us. I'm kind of glad you didn't. I always liked that you didn't seem to have the killer instinct."

"I hate him, Peter. Sometimes I have so much hate for him I don't know what to do with it."

Peter sat down on the couch, being careful not to step into any of the blood splatters. "Fred, I need you to talk to me for a minute, okay? We need to get things straight. Okay, now I'm sorry I lost my temper with you before. I know I've hit you in the past and you have every reason to be a little scared of me. Fred, I know you did this."

"But—"

Peter managed to stay calm, though his eyes were dark. "I don't want to hear it. Now look at me. Damn it, look at me, Fred. Listen. I think I can make this work out for the both of us. I have a plan that if it works we can not only get rid of this body but do something else we've both been itching to do. But you gotta be honest with me, my brother. Do you know how many low-life murderers I know? I deal with them every day. I mean think about it, Fred. I'm a hitman for fuck's sake. I'm exactly what Daddy raised me to be. What that means is that I have good eyes for things. When someone kills someone they get a certain look in their eyes. In some people it's something animal-like. Something feral. In others it's a guilty look. I think you got a little of both."

"Peter—"

"I'm not done yet, Fred. There are not a lot of things in this world I care about. You might be the only person on this planet. We went through the same childhood together, remember? Believe me, I know how bad it fucks a man up. The difference between me and you is this, in my opinion. I gave up early. I gave into the killer in me, you know? We both have this in us. Daddy gave it to us. Now, I'm going to ask you a question. And I want you to be fucking honest with me because I am all you got. Why did you kill this whore?"

"I don't know," Fred said. He looked down and into the dead girl's eyes. "I don't know."

Peter put his hand on top of Fred's. "Now we're getting somewhere. Now, I'm not mad at you for lying. I came in here ready to swing and you were already upset enough. I just wish you would have trusted me enough to tell me the truth straight up. Just tell me what happened."

"I went to the bathroom just to clean up a little. I was gone all of forty-five seconds. I peeked out at her through a crack in the door just to see if she was okay and I seen her looking through my journal. I fucking lost it, Peter. I grabbed the knife from the kitchen and told her to get the fuck out. That's when she went fucking nuts on me and started screaming. She wouldn't shut up. I'm sorry I didn't tell you immediately but I was scared. Don't tell Daddy."

"Heh. She wouldn't shut up so you decided to stick a kitchen knife in her mouth? It wasn't easier to tell her to get the fuck out? You're more like Pop than you think."

"Don't even joke about that. Don't ever say that again. Will you help me get rid of her?"

"Yep. And you're going to help me get rid of someone too. A fair trade. I was trying to figure out how to do it right this week and now this falls into my lap."

"What the hell do you mean?"

"Remember that conversation we had years ago? The one about getting some payback for Mom? I want to kill Daddy, Fred. I've had it with him. He's out of fucking hand. You remember my friend Kamal? Daddy whacked him this week. Didn't even fucking talk to me about it. I had to find out about it from Frankie. You believe that? Good old smiling Kamal and Daddy killed him. I've had it."

"I think one murder is enough for me, Peter. As much as I want Daddy dead, I don't think I have the stomach to kill him. I don't want to get involved in family politics. You know I don't. I never did."

"Answer this question with one word, Fred. I deserve this much. Do you want Daddy dead or alive?"

"Dead. But if I wanted to be the one to kill him, Peter, I would have killed him ten years ago when Mom died."

"Hear me out. If we do this right, we can even get Daddy to help dig his own grave. If I call him up and tell him we need him here, he'll come. Regardless of all that's happened, he loves us in his own twisted kind of way. We're all he's got. Normally, he would send someone else to help with something like this, but this is personal. This is family. He'll want to keep this between us and not make it a big thing. He doesn't trust anyone enough in the organization to get rid of bodies at the moment, not since George Grimm got whacked. He has me getting rid of fucking bodies now like some goddamn underling. He admitted he killed Mom, you know. About a year ago when he was drunk off his ass. He was laying on the floor crying like a baby about how he shot her."

Fred froze. "He didn't! I knew it, Peter! I fucking knew it! You always told me he loved Mom too much to do it, but I always knew he did it!"

"You gonna be part of this?"

"Tell me what you have planned."

"Simple. I'll get hold of Daddy and get him to come down here and give us a hand. He'll help us go down and get rid of the body if I play all the cards right. All I have to do is trump up like this is a family thing. He'll like that. We'll make him think you want to be with us now. He'll definitely help out if he thinks that. We'll go out into the woods and dig a big hole. Then we'll shoot the old man and bury him with the junkie whore. It's almost fitting."

"I don't think it will work, Peter."

"Of course it will work, Freddy. Daddy has no fear of us. I just wish we would have done this when we were kids. It would have saved us both a lot of trouble. Hell, I'm certain we'd both be doing something legit with our lives if Daddy hadn't of fucked us up. As soon as we get our story situated here, I'm going to call the old man. You won't even have to do nothing. I'll kill the fucker. All's you have to do is help me bury him. I'm gonna give you a gun just in case, though."

Peter paced back and forth, eyes never leaving the clock. Fred continued staring at the corpse of the woman, licking his lips. They had planned everything out as carefully as possible. Their father was on his way down and he wasn't very happy. He had only just managed to get to sleep when he got the phone call from his sons.

Headlights cut across the room and both men made nervous eye contact. Daddy was here.

"You let me do most of the talking, Fred, you hear?" Peter asked. "Daddy is fucking smart and he'll pick up on anything weird. Whatever he asks you, you tell him the fucking truth."

"I have a bad feeling about this, Peter," Fred said, standing up. "I haven't seen Daddy in five years. I don't even know how to talk to him anymore."

"You can do it, Freddy. I know—"

There was a hard thump on the front door. Peter walked over, peeked in the peep hole, and opened the door.

John O'Rourke stepped into the room. He appeared smaller dressed so casually—a blue t-shirt and a pair of jeans. Normally, he was wearing Armani suits. His black hair was cut short, patches of gray sprinkled throughout. His eyes, a striking blue, scanned the room calmly. He made brief eye contact with both sons before taking a long look at the corpse on the floor.

"I always knew you had a killer in you, Freddy," John said, grinning at the corpse. "A brutal one, too. Damn, you didn't even bother taking the knife out of her mouth." He outstretched his arms. "Come give your old man a hug."

"Hi, Daddy," Fred said, staring at his father for a few seconds before looking away. "Thank you for coming to help me out."

"What, you're not gonna hug the old man?" John said, smile fading. "Gonna leave me hangin' here? You want my help but you can't even touch me?"

Fred walked over and hugged his father.

John embraced him fiercely.

"You gained some weight, Freddy," John said, letting his son go and patting his stomach. "It's good to see you again, though. Real good. Believe it or not, I missed you." He walked over to the corpse and leaned down. "Well, this is a regular family gathering if I ever did see one. Nothing like a rotting corpse with a knife in her fucking mouth to bring us all together, eh boys? Let's do this is fast as possible and get it done. It's already almost midnight. We need to get her into the ground before sunrise."

"That's it?" Freddy asked, ignoring the look of panic Peter shot him.

"Yes, that's it, Freddy," John said, letting his voice drop down the dangerous whisper he was known for. "I realize we haven't had time to catch up, but we got a corpse on the floor here. There's plenty of time for playing catch-up after all is said and done. We'll have coffee together in the morning."

"You don't even care why I killed her?" Fred asked.

"Should I?"

Fred thought about it. "I guess not."

"Keep an eye out for the road, Peter," John said, staring into the darkness ahead. The headlights illuminated the trees around them in a milky glow, shadows flickering through the branches.

"It's hard to see. It's not marked or nothing."

"Is that it there?" Peter asked.

They had been driving for about thirty minutes. The corpse was in the trunk, completely wrapped in plastic. Fred sat in the backseat, staring at his father's head.

"It's been a long time since I took part in an actual burial," John said, turning down the unpaved dirt road. "I'd say at least ten years. You know what's weird, Freddy? I've been thinking about you lately. I've been thinking about the way things used to be."

"It's best you don't go there, Pop," Fred said. "It will only get us arguing."

"Just hear me out," John said. "You know what I wonder sometimes? I wonder what our lives would be like if the family wasn't caught up in all this. Some sick part of me wants to live a life like that. No pressures. I bet we might actually be a close. I know you don't think I have it in me, Freddy, but I do. Some part of me envies that you were able to walk away from the family. I've always felt trapped myself. Even if I wanted to I couldn't get out now. Too much blood on my fucking hands, you know? I'm just glad to be able to help you now. I think this is the first time you've ever asked for my help. I can't deny it feels good. Real fucking good. I knew you'd need me sometime in the future."

"I knew you would help us, Pop," Peter said.

Fred said nothing. He turned around, shocked at how dark it was. As far as he could tell they had driven out of pure blackness. He couldn't even see a tree. The car lurched and he felt a little queasy.

"Okay, there is another offshoot road coming up," John said. He took the turn.

"It's dark as fuck outside tonight. Hope it doesn't rain. Okay, we go down this for a few minutes and we'll be at the old dumping grounds."

"How long have you been using this place?" Fred asked. He rolled down the window a crack, feeling relieved at the stab of cold air that hit his temples.

"We haven't used this place in years," John said, making eye contact with his son in the mirror. "That's how I know it's pretty safe. There's still some bodies out here undiscovered from the fucking seventies. Imagine that, there are some corpses out here in rotting leisure suits and bell bottoms. Last thing some of them might have heard is a Bee Gees falsetto. It's almost sad when you think about it."

"You always think like a twisted bastard, Pop," Peter said. "Who would even think of saying the shit you do?"

"I just see all the details is all," John said. "It's a good way of looking at the world. There's more to see." He stared into the mirror. "I missed you, Fred. I gotta admit it's strange, this night. I always told Peter here you didn't have the killer instinct. Part of me is glad I was wrong, son."

"I didn't mean to do it, Daddy," Fred said.

John snickered. "You hear that, Peter? The way he said it just then it almost sounded like he spilled a drink on one of your mother's rugs."

The car went silent at the mention of their mother. Peter turned and looked out into the dark trees while Fred looked down at his fingers angrily.

"Do you miss her, Daddy?" Fred asked, trying to make his voice sound nonchalant, though he was fighting the urge to punch the back of his father's head.

"Yeah, I do," John said.

Up ahead loomed a massive pile of dumped garbage. A few deer stood in the damp grass off to the left, frozen for a few seconds before scattering in different directions. Clouds of fog billowed through the trees as they vanished.

John stopped the car and turned to face his son. "You know, it's kind of funny, Fred. I haven't seen you years, huh? Now I haven't even been with you in an hour and we're burying a body together."

"Heh. It's almost like a Hallmark moment for sick fucks," Peter said. He glanced nervously at Fred, who was barely hiding his anger.

John snickered and cut the ignition. "You think like me, Peter. Okay, boys, let's get this over with. I'll carry the shovels and you carry the body. We'll just take it out in the woods and find a spot."

The men got out of the car and into the darkness. Only the sound of the crickets chirping could be heard. Both Peter and Fred were thankful for dark as it would help hide their body language from the ever alert eyes of their father.

Fred fingered the revolver his brother had given him. He knew he should be nervous but he somehow felt calm. Already the way he had murdered that girl felt like a bad dream he had had months ago. It was amazing to him how fast a life could degenerate. Only eight hours ago he felt like a normal citizen.

John opened the trunk and covered his nose with his sleeve. "Jesus Christ! I'll never get used to that smell. Good thing this ain't my car. It's Frankie's. Get her out of there, boys. Make sure none of her blood spills out, okay? Sometimes lining the trunk with plastic doesn't help worth a shit."

John reached in and grabbed the shovels then stood off to the side. Peter and Fred each grabbed an end of the body and hoisted it from the trunk.

"All right," John said. "She ain't that heavy, is she? We should try to get her buried at least a little ways into the woods. And we need to bury her relatively deep, too. We don't want some fucking animal digging her up and ruining a perfectly good burying ground, do we?"

Shadowy trees surrounded them, and the wind whistled softly through the branches. The sky had cleared up a bit and the half-moon could be seen peeking through a milky cloud.

"This spot is good," John said, dropping the shovels to the ground. The sound seemed loud in the quiet of the wilderness. "Okay, now that we have the body out here and away from all the people I can ask a couple of questions. Did you know her, Fred? I figure she's just a whore by the way she looks."

"No, I don't even know her name," Fred said. "She's just a prostitute I picked up. I caught her going through my stuff, and I lost my temper."

John clapped his son on the back. "You're just like your old man was back in the day. You let your anger get the best of you. I can help you with that. There are many ways of bringing yourself back in control. Come see me."

Fred, not really knowing what to say, picked up a shovel and started digging. John stood and watched him, face half in shadow. Peter soon followed suit.

"You know, it makes me proud to stand here and watch you two do this," John said.

"Pop, could you please stop with all this I'm so proud of my sons bullshit, please?" Fred finally said. The sentence stayed in the air for a few seconds, loud in the quiet of the breeze and crickets. When John said nothing, the brothers started digging again.

"You are one ungrateful fat fuck, you know that, Freddy?" John finally said, his voice a low whisper. "I'm out here putting my ass on the line for you and you immediately start acting like you used to. Who killed this dead whore here, me or you? You trying to say you're better than the old man? That you have some higher ground to stand on? Well, why don't you look at it this way. The people I've killed are people that had it coming. I've never killed a single person that didn't bring it upon his or herself. Most of them lived a lifestyle just like me. What about you? You think this girl deserved a fucking knife in her? She's just a simple girl that went down the wrong path. She was just someone trying to survive. Just a tired old whore. And you cut her up. She barely looks twenty."

Peter kept digging. There was something in the voice that seemed dangerous. He tried to make out his father's expression but all he could see was a sliver of his shadowed face.

"Yeah, Dad, you're a regular angel," Fred said. "You really kid yourself like this? That there is some sort of gray area to murder? I don't kid myself. I know I fucked up. And you know what? When I look deep down into my soul I don't try to rationalize anything. It's only been a few hours since I killed her and already she's haunting my fucking head, okay. I don't like the way this feels. And I know I'm going to burn in hell. Just like you."

"Maybe I should leave right now," John said. "Leave you stranded out here with a corpse."

Fred pulled the gun from his pants. "How about this?"

"You little fuck!" John screamed. "Put that down now! You

just gonna stand there and let your brother do this to your old man, Peter?"

"I'm gonna help him," Peter said, dropping his shovel. He pulled out his own gun, cocking it at his chest before aiming it at his father's head.

"Why?" John asked.

"Got any jokes to make now, Pop?" Fred asked. "You're going to spend the next few months decomposing alongside this 'tired old whore'."

"Fuck you, Freddy," John said. "I won't give you the satisfaction of begging for my life. If your brother wasn't standing there holding a gun I wouldn't even be afraid of you. You don't have the fucking guts to do anything on your own. What, you don't think I know your brother is the one with the balls to do this?" He turned his dark face to Peter. "Is Kamal really worth this, Peter? That bastard was a snitch."

"He wasn't a snitch, Pop," Peter said. "You paranoid bastard. He loved working for you."

"That's what you think, Peter," John said. "I heard different. And my instincts told me something as well. I can't afford to take chances. I know you were close to him, but if my instincts were right he'd sink us all. You should stand on the side of your father, not on some nigger you just met a year ago. How fucking dare you."

"Just shoot him, Peter," Fred said. "I don't think I can stand another second of him."

"You shut the fuck up!" John shrieked. "I'll fucking—-"

Fred pulled the trigger.

John fell backwards, blood spraying from his neck, a shocked hiss of air escaping his lips. He lay covered in shadow, coughing.

Peter stepped forward and leaned over his father. "I'm sorry, Pop," he said before firing his own gun three times.

The two brothers stood in the darkness over their father's corpse. The wind had stopped and the only sound was their heavy breathing.

"This doesn't feel as good as I always hoped it would," Fred whispered. "Two people are dead because of me."

"I'm sorry, Fred," Peter said, tucking the gun back in his pants. "We better get to digging. We only have a few hours before the sun comes up. You better give me that gun back. I'm gonna clean them off and throw them with the bodies. They can't be tied to me anyway. Daddy's the one who gave them to me in the first place."

Fred picked up a shovel and started digging. "How do you feel about it?"

"Heh. I'm not even sure yet. I wanted that bastard dead for a long time but I can't say I feel great. Daddy was good to me sometimes."

"Did you love him?"

"Not at all. I don't think he loved us, either."

Fred thought about that. He had tried his whole life to be the opposite of his father. Within a space of hours he had come to see a part of himself he had always fought.

Fuck you, Daddy, he thought as he continued stabbing the earth with his shovel.

UNDENIED

DARK HOLLOW: FALL

Carverton — 1890

"There he goes," William Bryerly whispered, watching the cloaked figure.

The man's shoes clicked as he walked across the wet cobblestone street, his shadow looming impossibly big by the gas lamplight. His dark coattails sounded like the wings of a bird as they fluttered in the cool breeze. A horse and carriage could be heard off in the distance, the hooves clapping in steady rhythms.

"We should follow him into the cemetery this time," Joseph said, his breath fogging off into the cool night air.

The boys watched until the man vanished around the corner and then broke into a run. The fog-covered streets of Carverton were often quiet by this time of night, most of the townspeople retiring for the evening. William and Joseph had escaped from the windows of their bedrooms and into the massive oak tree that separated their houses. On most nights, they could be heard talking to each other from their rooms—the windows only yards away.

"We better hurry up or we're going to lose him," William said, already walking ahead but hiding in the shadows.

The night watchmen were everywhere in the last few weeks. A young doctor by the name of Ryan Harker had been found murdered in his home, his throat cut from ear to ear. Local prostitutes had also been found murdered recently. The boys knew if they were caught, they would most likely be grounded for months.

William and Joseph had been following the mysterious man for weeks. They had been lurking outside the gates of Dark Hollow Cemetery looking for ghosts one evening when they heard the footsteps from (in?) the darkness. Not wanting to be caught, they climbed a tree near the iron fence and waited.

The figure had come out of the night, fog trailing behind, his tall frame covered in black clothing. William could see the man wore a goatee and was bald, although it was impossible to tell how old he was.

The man stopped at the arched gateway of the cemetery, studying the twin angels that resided on both sides of the stone entrance. He sighed and entered, the wind whipping his long coat as if on cue. William was afraid of the wind, as he and Joseph had discovered that it always rushed you the second you entered the graveyard. Even in the daylight, it frightened him considerably. Although Joseph laughed when he suggested it, William was convinced the wind gusts were ghosts.

William found himself thinking about cemetery ghosts as they followed the enigmatic man down the shadowy streets. If anyplace was haunted, it was Dark Hollow. Only weeks ago, a popular poet by the name of Jacob Atherton hung himself within the gates of the graveyard. Earlier that month, they had also buried a murdered prostitute there as well, guaranteeing the cemetery would be haunted as far as William was concerned. If you added all the dead children that had turned up on the lake shore last summer, one could consider the cemetery the center of a ghostly universe.

As predicted, the man left the street and turned down a dirt road that led toward Dark Hollow. The boys followed, moving through the damp night. They watched as the man entered the cemetery gates and vanished into the fog.

The boys climbed the gate and entered the graveyard. Headstones jutted out of the fog, the marble glowing in the milky moonlight. Crickets heralded their arrival loudly. William was terrified, for he could not see the ground, and kept imagining the skeletal hands of the dead reaching from their graves and clutching at his feet. Joseph did not appear scared, his thick eyebrows arching as he looked around for signs of the mysterious man.

"I don't see him," William whispered, shivering as he pulled his coat around his tiny frame.

"The windows of that mausoleum are glowing." Joseph pointed into the misty darkness. "See it?"

William let his gaze follow his friend's finger and saw a gleaming window off in the distance. It was one of the larger mausoleums, a relatively recent one. Moving stealthily, the fog surging around their tiny forms, they approached the large tomb.

A light flickered in the mausoleum window, indicating a single candle flame. Soft voices came from inside.

William put his ear up to the thick door, eyes widening above his open mouth.

"I love you, Nathan," a young female said from within the mausoleum, her voice reverberating and echoing around the stone walls.

"You have no idea how much I missed you, Anna," a man said. "I see you every time I close my eyes. I hear your voice in every sound."

"I do not like this place, Nathan. It is cold and lonely. I want to be with you."

"I will take you from here soon, my love. It has to be done very carefully. If we are caught, they may not let us stay together. Sunday evening would probably be the best."

"But that is still five days away."

"I will come and visit you every night, Anna. I promise."

"Let's get out of here," William hissed.

The boys exited the arched gateway, their eyes darting back into the fog. It was as if they feared the older man was going to leap from graveyard and drag them inside.

"Who was he talking to?" Joseph asked.

"I don't know. You think it was a ghost?" William asked, running his hands through his blonde hair.

"It sounded like it. It sounded like she stays in there all the time. She said it was cold and lonely. Why can't she leave?"

"I'm going home. We can talk about it there. What if he comes out while we are standing here?"

The next morning the boys felt much braver. They stood before the gateway of Dark Hollow, staring up at the twin angels with wide eyes, as if the statues would swoop down upon them. The graveyard looked much friendlier by day—most of the menace devoured by the light of the blazing sun.

"Are we really going to do this?" William asked, his chubby cheeks flushed as he stared into the rows of chalky tombstones.

"Of course we are," Joseph said. His dark hair stuck out from his scalp in unruly points.

Taking deep breaths, they walked through the archway. William could not help but notice the way the wind promptly rushed through his hair like ghostly fingers.

In front of the mausoleum was carved the name:

Anna Wilde
1871-1891
Sadly missed by her husband, Nathan Wilde

It was a newer structure, but green lichen had already begun to grow around the base of the stone. Dead flowers surrounded a walkway that led to the entrance, some of them brown with decay, just a hint of the color of their former glory. A thick door, melancholic angels carved deeply into the dark wood, loomed ominously.

"That's the name we heard last night, Joseph. He called her Anna."

"Are we going to go in?" Joseph asked, though it was easy to see he did not want to go in at all.

William grinned, feeling much more courageous than he had last evening. "I don't think we have a choice. This is a mystery even Sherlock Holmes would be proud to solve."

Reaching out tentatively, William pushed on the door, surprised when it opened with a reluctant groan. He was certain it would be locked. Frowning, he turned back to face his friend. "We better hope Nathan doesn't come while we are here. If it's unlocked, he may be lurking about."

"If you keep lingering like this, he will," Joseph said, pushing him forward.

The stone crypt smelled of mildew and decay. A sliver of sunlight sliced over the room and directly across the cherry oak coffin that rested on a pedestal in the center. Dust motes swam through the sunlight and over the wooden chair that sat next to the casket. A table, a single lit candle on its smooth surface, sat against the wall. William shivered as he imagined the older man sitting in the chair by candlelight, talking to his ghostly wife.

"Are we going to open it?" Joseph asked, staring at the casket as if he expected it to fly open and spring forth a corpse.

"I suppose," William whispered, walking ahead, happy he could feel the sunlight burning into his back. He knew he would never be able to do such a thing by the light of the moon. He stepped on the chair as he was too small to open the coffin from where he stood. Reaching out carefully, William pulled at the lid.

A rush of foul air blasted into William's face, and he would have fallen from the chair had Joseph not steadied him. The corpse of Anna Wilde was well preserved, her porcelain face gleaming with an oily sheen. Her lips were blood red. Dark hair surrounded her face and rested over her shoulders in silky strings. A white dress covered her small frame, the folds fitting perfectly to her lithe figure. Her hands were crossed on her chest, long red nails protruding out from delicate fingers.

Though he wanted to leave, William reached out to touch her face, his hand shaking.

Anna's skin was hard and cold. Though she looked as if she could sit up at any moment, she was most definitely dead.

"You want to see her?" William asked, jumping down from the chair.

Joseph climbed up and studied the corpse for a few seconds before turning away, his face pale. "Let's get out of here."

Before leaving the crypt, they closed the coffin, dust motes swirling violently in the sunbeams. They retreated to the back of the cemetery to speak, sitting on the gravestone of a woman by the name of Lydia Rose.

"It had to be a ghost," William said, watching a crow from where it perched in a nearby tree.

"Maybe he met a woman in there," Joseph suggested, his eyes betraying his fear.

"And her name was Anna, too? The way she talked to him it sounded like it was her. And you know what is even more terrifying?"

"What?"

"Nathan is going to take her corpse out of there on Sunday."

"I think we should go to the authorities. Let them know what is going on."

"Would Sherlock Holmes go to the authorities?"

Joseph grinned. "Breaking into a mausoleum and overhearing a conversation does not make you Sherlock Holmes."

"I feel like Sherlock Holmes. Aren't you just the least bit curious? If we get any adults involved we won't be able to find out what happens. We could always contact them after we find out what he's going to do with the corpse. What if he can somehow bring her back alive?"

"Nonsense. I'd believe it was a ghost before I would believe he can bring her back from the dead."

"She sure was beautiful. She was young, too."

"Hello, boys," a man said from behind them.

Nathan Wilde's goatee was sprinkled with gray. His dark eyes glittered above his hollow cheeks. Smiling grimly, he removed his black derby, revealing his bald head.

"Why do you lurk about in the cemetery on such a nice day?" Nathan asked, rubbing his long fingers over his skull. "One would think you would have something better to do."

"And why are you here, then?" Joseph asked boldly in the same tone as the older man. "One would think the park would be a better place for a walk."

Nathan studied the boys for a few seconds before speaking, ebony eyes glimmering in the sunken confines of his face. "I've come to see my wife. She passed, God bless her soul. I come to see her every day." He paused and stared sadly. "You have no idea how much I miss her." He moved forward and leaned into Joseph's face. "You should enjoy your youth, my friend. The world gets much uglier with age. The cemetery is no place for the young—even in death."

Joseph backed away, nearly stumbling over a headstone. "Let's go, William."

"Take care, boys," Nathan called after them, placing his derby back upon his head.

Later, the boys sat on the shore of Lake Angel, watching the sun as it slowly vanished into horizon. Golden colors shifted on the surface of the water in dancing sparks. A warm breeze gently rushed through their hair, sending a pleasant smell of decaying flowers into their noses. William took a deep breath, enjoying the moment.

"I think we should follow him Sunday," Joseph said, his face glowing in the orange light of the setting sun.

"Two things can happen—both of which will leave me scared out of my mind," William said. "One, he can leave the crypt with a ghost. Two, he can leave the crypt with her corpse. Either way, I'll have nightmares for the rest of my life. I'm already starting to have nightmares as it is."

"Nathan Wilde was strange. When I was five, I saw a man in the city get taken to the asylum. Nathan's eyes looked like his."

On Sunday night, the boys went to the Wilde mausoleum, hiding in a tree only yards away from the stone steps. Dead leaves fell around them, dragging against the bark as they dropped to the ground in dry whispers.

William concentrated on the full moon through the skeletal branches of the tree, watching his breath fog up into the starry sky. He wondered if this was the same tree the local poet had hung himself from.

It was just past midnight when the old man arrived on the steps of the crypt, his heels clicking the stone steps as he approached the door.

"I have come, my love," Nathan said, pushing the door open with a creak and walking inside.

"Let us leave immediately, Nathan," a female voice said from inside the crypt.

William and Joseph froze where they perched within the

branches, both of them wanting to scream. They had checked the mausoleum when they arrived, and the only thing inside was Anna's corpse.

"We must be careful, Anna," Nathan said, his voice echoing from the stone structure and out into the graveyard. "If they should find us before we get home, I fear we will never see each other again."

When Nathan walked outside of the crypt doors, Anna clutched stiffly in his arms like a piece of wood, William had to swallow the squeal that threatened to fire from his throat. Rigor mortis held Anna straight, her body rigid and stiff. Black hair flowed down from her head, waving behind her in the chilly breeze. The rancid smell of decay wafted upwards, stabbing into their nostrils in sickly sweet waves.

"Say nothing until we get home, Anna," Nathan hissed and vanished into the looming tombstones, the wispy fog swirling around his form as if he had been consumed.

The boys waited almost a half-hour before they found the nerve to climb down from the tree.

For the rest of the week, the boys were assailed by mountains of schoolwork and had little time to follow up on the doings of Nathan and Anna Wilde. Truth be told—they really were too scared to return to their mystery. William dreamt every night of Anna's stiff body clasped tightly in Nathan's arms.

They learned from some of the local gossip that Nathan Wilde, an older doctor, had married young Anna only a year ago. They had been very much in love. Nathan was devastated when his wife had died of pneumonia only six months after their wedding.

It was almost two weeks later when William and Joseph found themselves watching Nathan stroll across the walkway of his home and down the road toward the town. When they could no longer hear his footsteps, they crept into his backyard and tried the door. It was open.

The kitchen was clean and modest. A large bowl of fruit sat in the center of the table. Joseph snatched an apple as they passed, ignoring the withering look he got from William.

The rest of the house also appeared normal, almost religiously clean. The only place they had not looked was the closed bedroom door on the second floor. William looked back at Joseph before opening the door, his body tense and ready to run away at the first sign of movement.

Turning the handle cautiously, his breath held in his lungs, William pushed open the door.

Anna lay in the center of the bed, her round face protruding from her dress like a meticulously created doll, an odd smile on her thin lips. Dark hair flowed from her head, making her pale face loom like a moon within the folds of her red sheets. Her eyes were open, but stared upwards to the ceiling, focusing off into nothing.

The boys circled the bed with soft footsteps, eyes wide above their open mouths. They stopped only when they were inches away from her curiously fake metallic face.

"She's smiling," William whispered.

"If she moves I will die. I swear it," Joseph said, his voice trembling.

His hand shaking, William reached out and touched the corpse's nose. Anna's entire face shifted downwards as if it was collapsing, and he squealed and pulled backwards.

"Her face moved!" William hissed.

"I think it's a mask," Joseph said, pointing at the side of her head. "See?"

William placed his finger on the edges of Anna's face and pushed it upward. Underneath was the real Anna Wilde—her skin gray and mottled, her eyes sunken deep within her face.

"You really think she talks?" William asked, putting the mask back.

"I don't know. We both heard her."

They heard the front door open, followed by the clicking of shoes against the wooden floor.

"Oh, God," William hissed, his terror filled eyes darting around the room for an escape. "What are we going to do?"

Joseph was already rushing to hide behind the thick curtain, his thin frame instantly vanishing within the azure folds.

William leapt into the wardrobe, closing the door just as Nathan walked into the room.

"I was going to go into town, Anna, and get us some more wine…but I was drawn back to you," Nathan said.

William managed to get his eye to the crack in the door and peered out into the bedroom. Nathan was sitting on the bed, his hand running lovingly over Anna's shoulder.

"I knew you would not be gone long, Nathan," Anna said. "You never are."

From where William was hiding, he could not see Nathan's face. Because of the mask, he could not tell if Anna was speaking, but the thought she might be nearly made him wet his pants.

Nathan began to remove his clothes, black pants falling to his pale ankles. He slid onto the bed, his hands running up the folds of his dead wife's dress and over her leathery chest. His breath quickened in lustful gasps.

"Make love to me, Nathan," Anna whispered.

Moaning, Nathan pulled his dead wife's dress upwards, rolling between her bluish-black legs. He thrust himself forward, passionately kissing the mask. William let his eyes drift to Anna's perpetual smile, his numb mind nearly snapping as he watched her doll-like head shift up and down.

"I love you, Nathan," Anna said as her husband's hand ran lovingly over her dark hair.

With a final violent sigh, Nathan lunged forward, eyes clamped shut on his flushed face. Teardrops fell down his cheeks in glistening lines. "I love you, too."

Joseph ran from his hiding place in the curtains, passed Nathan in a shrieking blur, and fled down the stairs. Nathan leapt from the bed, throwing on his clothes.

"There is another in the wardrobe, Nathan," Anna whispered.

William felt hot urine spill down his leg and into his shoe.

"What are you doing?" Nathan asked, wrenching open the wardrobe door.

"They are not doing anything, my love," Anna said. "They are just curious boys."

For a brief moment, William actually thought the corpse spoke, but realized quickly that Nathan had, in fact, said the words.

Nathan stared down at his wife. "And you let me make love to you while they watched?"

"My mind is not what it used to be, Nathan. When you entered the room I lost touch again, forgetting everything. I told you it happens sometimes. I did not remember until the boy ran by."

Nathan closed the door and leaned backward, his eyes wet with tears. "Please do not ruin this for me. We just want to be left alone. We aren't hurting anybody." His voice fell to the whisper of Anna Wilde, his whole body taking on feminine idiosyncrasies. "You worry too much, Nathan. These boys won't tell anyone. They are scared."

William just stared at the old man speechlessly, a soft hiss escaping his open mouth. He had no idea how to reply to something so surreal. He was not sure if he was dealing with a lunatic, or a man possessed by the spirit of his dead wife— either one was ghastly.

"You must promise me you will leave us be," Nathan continued in his own voice. "I will only let you leave if you promise. I will *not* be denied the love of my wife."

"I promise," William said, wondering if he would survive a fall from a second story window should he choose to jump.

"Let him go," Nathan said in Anna's voice. "He is only a baby."

"Please, sir, let me go," William pleaded. "I promise we won't tell anyone. We'll never come back."

"What about the other? Will he tell?"

"He may if I don't get to him in time. I promise you, I will stop him."

Nathan blinked, eyes screaming with madness. Then, the air rushed from his body as if he was defeated. He moved from the door and threw himself upon his wife, embracing her corpse as he wept.

William rushed down the stairs and toward the back door. The last thing he heard as he exited the house was Nathan's sobbing.

Later that night, the boys talked from the windows of their bedroom. "I don't want to tell," William said, staring at his friend's face in the candlelight. "He's not hurting anybody."

"He's mad, William," Joseph said. "Who knows what the man is capable of. We need to tell."

"You didn't see him. He was embracing her and weeping when I left. It bothered me. He's a lonely and sick man."

"He's a dangerous man. Who is to say he will not come up here and kill us next? Put us into his house somewhere like some horrifying doll."

"Is that how people make babies?" William asked.

"I don't know. I don't think Anna is going to be making any babies anytime soon."

They both snickered despite how much the image still pierced into their minds.

"I just realized something, Joseph," William whispered, his fingernails digging painfully into the flesh of his leg.

"What?"

"Anna told him where I was."

"He speaks for her, fool. He talks with her voice—he's mad."

"No, Joseph. Anna told him I was in the closet. How could she have known unless she really is speaking through him?"

The boys said nothing, both of them knowing their sleep would be plagued by nightmares of Anna Wilde's eerie doll-like smile.

By the end of the week, neither of the boys had told anyone of their adventure at the Wilde house. Perhaps they feared what Nathan would do to them, or perhaps they did indeed take pity on the poor old man.

It turned out they did not have to tell anyone after all.

Nathan Wilde, possibly fearing the boys would tell what he had done, poisoned himself. The authorities found his body in the bed with his wife's decayed corpse, his arms clutched around her in a tight embrace, a ghostly smile on his face.

Years later, William was told that Nathan had implanted a tube of some sort between Anna's legs to aid in intercourse. He listened to the tale with a shudder, remembering vividly the way the old man had plunged himself passionately into his dead wife.

William often thought of Nathan as he grew older. Within

time, his revulsion had transformed to pity. He wondered if he would ever love someone as much as Nathan loved Anna, and in that regard, he even felt a pang of jealousy. For Nathan Wilde, even God could not deny him his love for his wife.

FEELING ALIVE

"Need a ride?" Earl asked, offering the hitchhiker a smile even though he probably could not see it in the dim interior of the '74 Chevy.

"Thank you," the man said, his voice deep and gravelly—the kind of voice of one who has seen a lot of the world.

When the door opened, Earl was able to get a better look at the hitchhiker. He was wearing a denim jacket, buttoned closed over his wiry frame. Old acid washed jeans clung tightly to his bony hips, splatters of oil and dirt covering the legs. A zapata style mustache rested so thin on his lips it appeared to have been painted on with the edge of a magic marker. His eyes were expressive—almost haunted, the sort of eyes that one got after coming home from a particularly brutal war. Three scar lines snaked across his left cheek, nearly touching the corner of his almond-shaped eye.

"I've been trying to get a ride for the last two hours," the hitchhiker said gruffly, his voice seeming to rumble and vibrate. "It just isn't as easy as it used to be." The man offered a warm, clammy hand. "My name's Saint."

Earl took the hand. "I'm Earl. Did you say Saint? Like in Saint Christopher?"

"Yeah. But it don't mean anything religious to me. My mother was a religious person. She figured she couldn't go wrong with a name like Saint. She figured wrong, may she rest in peace. Nice to meet you, Earl. It's good to see that there are people around who will still pick up hitchhikers."

Earl nodded, running his fingers habitually over his shaven head. "Not a problem, my friend. I used to travel the land myself. When I turned eighteen, I pulled a Jack Kerouac. Traveled all over the place for two years. I soaked America in like a sponge. I remember standing on a dark road just like this watching tiredly as one car after another passed me by. I sort of miss those days."

Saint pulled out a cigarette from his shirt pocket and looked over at Earl. "You mind if I light this?"

"Not at all. Used to smoke myself."

"Used to? I have no idea how you managed to quit. I'd rather die than give up my cigarettes."

"I used to feel the same way," Earl said, inhaling deeply of the second hand smoke that trailed from Saint's cigarette. "So what you gonna do for the end of the world?"

"Eh?" Saint grunted, blowing smoke from the side of his mouth. He was staring at the yellow line in the center of the road as if it somehow hypnotized him.

"The end of the millennium, my friend. In about twenty minutes that big ol' ball is going to drop over at Times Square."

Saint laughed and turned to face his new companion. "You may not smoke cigarettes, Earl, but you must be smoking something. I don't know what year you're in, but it's the year 2000. We went through all that shit last year."

"That's what most people think, but technically, the year 2001 is the start of the next millennium."

Saint nodded, taking another long puff from his cigarette. "Yeah. I think I read about that somewhere." He exhaled trails of smoke through his nose, his face somber. "Forgot about it. Ain't nothing going to happen anyway. It's just another year."

"I suppose. But you never do know. Do you just hitchhike all over, or do you have a particular destination?"

"I never know where the hell I'm going, man. I just travel all over the place and soak in America. Soak it all up in its blood and glory." Saint patted his hefty backpack. "Then I record it all in here. When I die, anyone gives a fuck, they can read it with their eyes wide and their open mouth resting on their chest."

Earl let his eyes fall down to the backpack. "Some shocking stuff in that book, huh?" He smiled lecherously. "Ever meet any women on the road?"

Saint looked over to see if he was being mocked and relaxed when he saw the lust in Earl's eyes. "Sure I do. Lots of them."

"You fuck any of them?"

"Sometimes I do."

Earl nodded, his eyes glistening. "I envy your freedom, my friend. There was a day when I used to travel the world like that. For a time, I lived by my own rules—my own laws." His voice dropped to a whisper. "Then I got locked up for a bit. They say it did me good, but I think it just sucked the fucking life out of me. I don't think I was crazy anyway. I miss the old days. Life was so exhilarating on the road."

"It *is* exhilarating." Saint looked over at Earl just as an incoming car's headlights sliced across the interior, and their eyes met. In that brief moment, as if through osmosis, they sensed a kindred soul within each other. "I'll be doing this until the day I die. Living by your own rules is living by the very nature of your being. Man was not made to live by laws. It's unnatural. It doesn't mean shit."

"See, I think that's where society is heading. By our very nature, we are nothing but animals. Laws merely hold us in place—sort of put a proverbial cage around us. If all laws ceased to exist at this moment, the world would be a fucking bloodbath. Survival of the fittest. What you do—what I used to do…is acknowledge that." Earl turned over and studied Saint, seeing him for what he really was. "Man is meant to follow his instincts. I think society is heading to a point where man will eventually see that the laws are meaningless and break the chains—become the predators that we are."

"What made you stop?" Saint asked. The question hung in the air for a brief moment, both of them knowing exactly what he was really asking, but neither of them sure if it would be safe to take off the mask.

Earl grinned. "I didn't stop, my friend. I only got more insidious. I've found that it's more fun if you can manipulate the very people you live around. People are sheep—you smile at them the right way, offer a touch in a perfect moment, say whatever the fuck you want them to hear—and they are instantly charmed. It's an invigorating feeling when they don't realize the monster is right in their midst. Ever hurt them first?"

Saint closed his eyes as if he had taken a shot of heroin. *"Oh yeah.* I usually do." He turned on the interior light above his head and unzipped his backpack, pulling a pearl handled straight razor from within the cluttered papers and dirty clothes. Splatters of blood could be seen on the edges of the blade. "See this? My pride and joy. I've used it so much it's almost like an extension of myself."

Earl studied the blade and nodded with admiration. "Were you going to kill me with that?"

"Yeah. Probably," Saint grinned, his eyes dancing with a mixture of controlled rage and glee. "But that was when I thought you were a—what did you call it? A sheep."

"I was going to kill you too. I don't think I've ever talked about this with anyone before. And on an even fucking stranger note—we've only known each for what? Ten minutes? I don't think I've ever felt so opened up with another human being before—when I looked into your eyes, I knew you would understand everything."

"Call it fate. Call it a New Years Eve present from God, his own bad self. It's sorta freeing to be honest. Hell, the only time I get to show my true self is just before I cut some bitch with my straight razor. For that moment, however brief it is for them, they get to see me for what I am." Saint paused for a moment, letting the smoke exit his nostrils in thin, serpent-like streams. "That makes me feel alive. I don't feel hidden in that moment... or invisible."

"I remember my first time. She couldn't have been any more than twenty. She was walking near the river dike and I was just behind her, sort of lost in my own thoughts. She stepped off the dike and went into the woods—a shortcut, I guess. I felt compelled to follow her. Ten minutes later, she was dead. Fucked and strangled." Earl nodded his head in grim satisfaction, then grinned wickedly. "And not necessarily in that order, if you know what I mean. That's why I got sent to the Asylum. I pretended like it was a Leprechaun named Ulysses that told me to kill that girl. On some days, I miss the fucking chaos of that place. The mood was so tense you felt like you were in an electrical vacuum. I had to manipulate the shit out of people to get out. "

Saint nodded his head knowingly. "I can't believe we're talking about this shit. I've spent my whole life in silence, knowing what I was but never saying shit. Then you come along, and I open up like a fucking loose hinged door. What the hell, man?"

"I know what you mean. I thought I would take all this shit to my grave. The only explanation I can give is that it was just meant to be. It seemed so natural, you know?" Earl grinned. "It was like we were put together by the Devil or something. A sort of New Years gift."

Saint snickered. "You just might be right, Earl. I spent my whole damn life praying to that horned fucker—dedicating a kill here or there to him. It's only right that I meet someone who understands me on what some whack-ass religious nuts think might be the end of the world. Maybe we're supposed to help the end come about or something."

"I see no reason to argue with you, my friend. When I woke up this morning, I knew something was different—something important. I kind of chalked it up to the fact that the new millennium was arriving, but with you here I see things in a different light. I think you're right. I'm ashamed of myself. Ashamed for letting myself stay docile for so long. I want my old life back. I'm sick of keeping this shit in check. I couldn't tell you how many times I had to fight the urge to pull back. I think everyone has this. Anyone who's ever wanted to rip the throat out of the man who just pulled out in front of you can understand this shit. They feel that instinct."

Up ahead, a giant billboard was flashing the time as 11:56, the numbers shimmering gaudily in the frigid winter air, an advertisement for a restaurant celebrating its birthday at the end of the New Year. A Lincoln Mercury was parked just underneath the sign, the garish billboard lights reflecting on the roof hypnotically. A man was on the right side of the car angrily turning a tire jack, his hot breath firing above his head in furious clouds.

Earl and Saint turned to face each other—neither of them

surprised to see a smile burning across their features with blistering sharpness.

"I've never done this with a partner," Earl said as they pulled right in back of the Mercury. "But I can't think of a better way to celebrate the next millennium."

The man turned to face them, his hand over his forehead in a vain attempt to block the blinding light from piercing his eyes. He instantly stood up, a nervous grin on his face as he ran his fingers through his wavy blonde hair apprehensively. Holding his hand out in a friendly gesture, he nodded. They could see the silhouette of a passenger on the right side of the car.

"Should be interesting," Earl whispered.

"Ain't you going to use a weapon?" Saint asked, caressing his straight razor like it was a favorite pet.

"Nope. Don't need one. I'll get the passenger; you get the other. Watch out for that tire jack."

Earl and Saint exited the car simultaneously.

Hiding his threatening body language, a skill Earl had learned from years of manipulation, he approached the car. "Howdy!"

Saint went off like a bomb, exploding forward with almost supernatural speed, the straight razor slicing through the air in a dizzying blur. The sound of paper ripping penetrated the silence and a crimson line appeared underneath the shocked man's chin. The victim's eyes widened, still blinded by the headlights and he stuck his hands over the cut as if he could possibly hold all that blood. The straight razor whirred through the air once again, piercing deeply into the side of the man's neck with a soft whisper. Arterial fluids sprayed into Saint's smile, dotting his face in red splatters. The man fell to the icy ground hard, still gasping as Saint brought his blade down yet again.

The woman was already screaming as Earl wrenched the passenger door open, his snarling teeth gnashing down into her lips like a rabid dog, his hands pulling her face into his from the back of her head. She continued to shriek—her cries wet from her blood soaked throat. Earl pulled her from the car by her neck, still chewing ravenously into her face, gnawing on cartilage and pulling back only when his teeth struck painfully into her howling skull.

By the time Earl pulled away, his feral face glimmering in the headlights, the woman had long ceased to move. Steam was smoldering from her mutilated face, rising upwards before being devoured by the chill.

"Jesus, man," Saint said, a droplet of blood falling from his chin. He had just cut the index finger of the man off and was placing it in his backpack. "When you say you don't need a weapon, you mean it, my friend."

Earl giggled, the laugh escaping his lips in a guttural growl of foggy breath, and looked up to the billboard. He whispered the last ten seconds to the new millennium, the words coming out of his mouth in blood tinged bursts. When the numbers reached midnight, he waited for a brief moment, wondering if the world would, in fact, end.

Earl looked over at Saint—his grinning teeth caked with the flesh of his victim. "Happy New Year, man. Feels fucking good to be alive."

THEY ALL DREAM ABOUT THEM HERE

"Ah, new cellmate? Hello there, pardner," a man's gravelly voice asked from a dimly-lit corner of the room.

I just stared at him as the cell door slammed shut at my back.

The man's face illuminated as he struck a match and lit his cigarette. He had a long nose and a face full of scars and lines. His two front teeth were unusually long and jutted out like a rodent. Messy blond hair stuck out from his head in stringy slivers. He gazed back at me, shadows dancing around his dark blue eyes. He finally waved the match out and studied me as he took slow puffs from his cigarette.

"Friendly, aren't ya?" the man finally asked.

I sighed and threw my extra set of clothes on the top bunk bed. The cell smelled of sweat and shit.

"Look, you don't gain anythin' by being rude to me," the man said, blowing smoke out of the side of his mouth. "My name is Robert, but you can call me Rabbit. Everyone else does. Even my own momma calls me Rabbit on account of my teeth. I know how to survive a place like this, so you should stay friendly with me. I've been here for ten years now." He held his hand out for shaking.

I stared at him a moment before speaking, ignoring his hand. "Listen, I spent two years in a Texas prison. I think I can handle a stay at this place. My name is Frank Morrison."

"Do you dream a lot, Frank?"

"What the hell kind of question is that? It's none of your damn business whether I dream or not."

"See, that's why I'm still sane," Rabbit whispered I couldn't stop staring at his teeth. "On account that I don't dream. I haven't dreamed in a long time."

"Listen, Rabbit," I said. "I don't care about your dreams, either. I just want to serve my time and get the hell out of here. I want to do it quietly with no trouble. Understand?"

"I don't dream on account of my brain damage. I shot myself in the head after murderin' my cheating wife. I found her in bed with a fuckin' Bible salesman. You believe that shit? I shot them both up real good. I regret it now, but what can you do? I must have shot away the part of my brain that dreams. Travis, my last cell mate, he was a dreamer. Dreamed every damn night. It drove him mad. He only died two days ago, you know. Bashed his head into the wall on your left there. See it? They cleaned it as best they can, but you can still see the splatters. I have more I want to tell you, but I don't know if I can trust you yet."

I looked to my left. The cell wall did indeed have what appeared to be a large blood splatter I could see droplets on the floor too. A fly buzzed in one of the darker areas Some guys do not handle prison well. I'd seen my fair share of men losing their minds when I was in the Gulf War. They get to the point where they will do anything to destroy themselves.

I turned back to face Rabbit.

He was smiling, teeth gleaming. "So you fought in the war, huh?" he asked. "You should be a hero. How did you manage to fuck things up so much that you ended up here? Life is almost funny the way things end up. Hell, you made the world a free place, and now you are stuck in a very small cell with a convicted murderer." His southern accent was so thick he almost sounded like a cartoon. He pronounced the last word "murderah." He was like a dangerous and feral Forrest Gump.

"What I'd like to do is get a little peace and quiet in here so I can get some sleep, Rabbit," I said. "Think you can handle keeping your mouth shut until morning?"

"I'm looking forward to gettin' a good night's sleep myself," Rabbit said as he laid back, arms behind his head. "Travis talked in his sleep. Anyway, I hope you're friendlier in the mornin'."

I didn't answer him as I removed my shoes and climbed into bed. I stared at the black ceiling and thought about my fate.

It was 1999, and if I played my cards right I should be able to get out of this place in about four or five years with good behavior.

I got sent here for robbery. Why? I guess you could say that the war fucked me up real bad. I had a hard time adjusting to regular life, and it wasn't long before I was struggling to make some cash. When the judge found out I was a veteran, it only seemed to make him meaner.

I was sent here, one of the world's most hardcore prisons. This prison was much worse than I expected it to be. It looked ancient for one thing. This place must have been built over a hundred years ago. The black-gray walls were covered with strange scratch marks. The lighting, a sickly fluorescent, was so dim you had to squint in many places.

The guards here also seemed odd. They had a strange zombie-like look about them, like their minds were other places. When they did look at you it was with a cold and murderous gaze. I hadn't seen one friendly face since I got here. The prison seemed like something out of the early 1900's. You would think Georgia would have all modern prisons by now. Last I heard they were building a new one, but that they wouldn't be moving the prisoners for another few years now.

The smell was something I didn't think I'd ever get used to. There was something just underneath all the damp mildew— something decaying.

It was also unnaturally quiet. Normally, a prison would be loud with all kinds of different noises—men laughing and shouting, guards giving orders, etcetera. Not one single prisoner shouted out at me as I was being led to my cell. I was greeted only by the same I-am-dead-inside eyes from all of them. It was like they were listening to a mysterious song that only they could hear. There was such a strong sense of despair about the whole place. It felt as if something was about to happen. There was a kind of tension in the air.

I fell asleep staring at the ceiling, imagining that I could somehow see the stars above

When I awoke, Rabbit was standing right next to me, staring into my face.

"They visited ya, Frank," Rabbit said. "And look, you're

bleedin' on the corner of your eye. What did you dream about?"

I jumped out of the bed and grabbed Rabbit by the throat, slamming him against the blood-splattered wall. "Stay away from me when I'm sleeping. In the future, if I say anything in my sleep I want you to keep it you yourself. I just want to do my time and get out of here. I don't want to make a friend of a brain-damaged, inbred, buck-toothed murdering fuck named Rabbit, you understand?"

As I let go of his throat I felt something wet drop down the side of my right cheek like a teardrop. A droplet of blood landed on my foot. I touched the side of my face and I felt a small burning spot where I was missing my flesh. My chest was burning too.

But I did dream. It was one of the most horrifying dreams I've ever had.

"I can help you, Frank," Rabbit said. His voice was raspy from being choked. "I know a lot about them. Travis told me all about them."

"What the hell are you talking about?"

"They walk on their knees," Rabbit said. He rubbed his throat as he moved to sit on the bed. "But they move with the grace of wild cat. They have long nails that scrape and click when they walk. Their faces look painted—almost like them Japanese geisha girls."

I froze. How the hell could he know? "What the fuck are they, Rabbit?"

"Travis called them the dream demons. They live in this prison."

"Your last cell-mate dreamed about them?"

"They all dream about them here, Frank. All except me. They dream about other things, too. Tell me what you saw in your dream, Frank. Maybe I can help ya."

I sighed. I didn't want to tell this crazy fucker anything about me. But something seemed too real about the dream. And as fucked up as my head was from the war, I knew there was just no way that my mind could dream up that thing. The only place that a thing like that could come from was Hell. Plus, how the hell could he know what they look like?

"If I find that you told any of the other prisoners about my dream I will choke you in your sleep," I finally said. "Do you understand, Rabbit?"

Rabbit offered me a smile, his blue eyes seeming to glow with excitement. "Tell me, Frank."

"It wasn't like a dream at all," I said, shuddering as I saw its eyes in my mind. "I was sleeping and I awoke to the sound of heavy breathing. I couldn't tell what it was at first so I waited a minute for my eyes to adjust. He had these long arms that bent in all kinds of weird directions. This fucking thing was stuck to the ceiling above me, hanging by his nails like a spider. What kind of sick bastard would create a being like this? Its face was white and it almost seemed like it was covered in some kind of thick make-up, red lipstick and black mascara. The mouth is painted in a smile, but the lips cover long, sharp teeth. The eyeliner looked Egyptian almost, like King Tut or some shit like that. He was just staring at me with these crazy eyes, not blinking." I stopped talking. I hadn't felt this unsettled for a long time.

"Keep goin', Frank," Rabbit said, nodding his head.

I continued "I tried to move, but I found that I was paralyzed. Then the thing dropped down on me. It just stared into my eyes. I could feel its hot hands on both of my sides. He leaned back and thrust his face right into mine. His breath smelled like flowers. He brought his sharp fingernail under my eye and just gave it a little cut. Then it cut my shirt away and started writing in my flesh. It was so goddamn real, Rabbit. It was the most painful thing I've ever been through. Not words, something else. They looked like symbols or hieroglyphics. After awhile, I couldn't even see the symbols anymore because there was too much blood. When it was done, it skittered back up the wall and literally disappeared into the ceiling. I still have fucking goose bumps here, Rabbit. If that was just a dream how the hell did that thing get in my head? I would never even in my darkest imagination create something like that."

I looked at my chest, expecting to see some of the strange markings. There was nothing, but I could still feel it burning my flesh.

"It wasn't really a dream, Frank," Rabbit said. He stood up and looked at the ceiling. I followed his line of sight and saw that the corner was unusually dark. Or maybe dark was the wrong word. It was more blurry, like it was underwater or something.

"I don't understand what you mean. My chest isn't bleeding. So how the hell is it not a dream?"

"Your eye, Frank," Rabbit said. "It's not still bleedin', but it was."

I stopped breathing for a second. "Holy shit, you're right. But how do I know you didn't cut me in my sleep?"

"And cause you to have a dream where somethin' cuts you?"

"I guess you are right."

A voice boomed into the cell from the corridor outside. A message from the warden. "There is a lockdown currently in progress. All men just hold steady. We will get breakfast to you as soon as possible."

"What the hell is that about?" I asked.

"They had one yesterday too," Rabbit answered. "John Manson was murdered in his cell. A man named Riley Walker was murdered last weekend. All cut up, they was—even though there wasn't a knife in sight. I'm sure you have a good idea what cut him, Frank, don't you? It was all this prison talked about yesterday. It must have happened again."

"Are you trying to tell me these dream demons as you call them are murdering people in their dreams, Rabbit?"

"No. They aren't quite doing it in dreams, Frank. They are real. I think that you can just see them better in your dreams. And not just the dream demons are killin' people. There are other things, too. They are just as unspeakable from what Travis told me."

"Why do you keep saying they aren't doing it in dreams."

Rabbit picked up a bar of soap from the sink and held it out to me. He smiled, his buck teeth appearing even larger. "Watch this. Travis and I discovered it a few weeks ago."

Rabbit threw the bar of soap right into the ceiling above his head. To my astonishment, the soap vanished with a soft pop.

I felt my goose bumps rise. "What the hell was that? Is this some kind of trick?"

"I told you it wasn't a dream. That's how that thing got into the cell. It's some sort of a doorway."

"A doorway to where, Rabbit?" I asked, still staring at the ceiling in disbelief. "How the hell is this possible?"

"A doorway to where they come from. I don't know how it's possible any more'n you do."

"Could we go in there?"

"I don't know. I've never tried. Why would you want to? You really want to come face to face with one of them in their own place?"

"I'd rather find some way to stop them before they visit me again," I said. As I spoke, I could still feel my chest burning.

A half-hour later our breakfast arrived. We ate in silence. I could not keep my eyes away from the blurry corner of the room. It was like my dream had somehow spilled into waking reality, though I knew that wasn't the case. Not if Rabbit's last cell mate had an encounter with these dream demon things.

After some arguing, I found myself sitting on my top bunk with a sheet tied around my waist. We had tied together a bunch of them, creating a makeshift rope. The plan was for me to venture into this damn invisible hole. I had already put my hand into it and nothing had happened other than a slight cold feeling on my fingertips. If the guards came in right now I wasn't sure how we would manage to explain what the hell we were doing.

"Remember, Rabbit, if you hear me cry out I want you to pull me back in," I said, readying myself mentally. "If you feel me tug on this I want you to pull me back in, too."

With a little help from Rabbit, I managed to poke my way into the hole.

All I could see in every direction was a sickly green mist. The cold air snapped into my face, smelling sweet, but with a sense of decay underneath. Off in the distance I could hear someone screaming. Seeing no immediate threat, I managed to climb all the way in. The sheet, still tied around my waist, disappeared into the green mist below my feet.

I walked as far as the sheet would allow, which was about eight feet. I couldn't tell which way was up, as the greenish mist covered everything. I couldn't even tell whether it was a ceiling or a sky above my head. What the hell could this place possibly be? The only words that came to my mind was from the old science fiction and horror magazines I used to read as a kid: Another dimension.

Off in the distance I could hear a soft clicking sound. And it was getting closer.

Click. Click. Click. Click.

I knew what it was immediately—one of the dream demons.

The space between the clicking sounds got faster and I could sense that it was coming right for me.

I was about to yank on the sheet to have Rabbit pull me back in when one of the demons flew out of the mist. I tried to jump to the side but only managed to lose my balance and fall backwards on my ass.

The demon sailed over my head, its geisha face painted into a grimace, and then seemed to vanish into the floor itself.

I waited a second, but nothing happened. Other than the occasional scream off in the distance, everything was quiet.

The dream demon had gone right into the cell with Rabbit. I gave the sheet a hard tug, and to my shock, it was loose. I pulled it again. Rabbit's end of the sheet was nothing but a blood-covered, frayed piece of sheet. I bit down panic as I fell to my knees and started crawling as fast as I could to the spot where I imagined the doorway to our cell was.

The demon shot out of the ground just in front of my face, spraying me with blood. It ran off into the mist, vanishing.

I stared at the spot where I saw the creature exit, and I fell forward into the cell. I landed on the top of the bunk bed and looked around. The bloodied end of the sheet still lay in the other world and hung from the ceiling as if it was embedded into the stone.

As a war veteran I have seen a lot of horror and carnage. So much, that I thought I was practically numb to it on some level. But what I saw educated me to a new way of seeing what violence could do.

Blood was splattered everywhere. Rabbit was literally

scattered all over the room. Pieces of his flesh clung to the wall and cell bars. The only recognizable part of my former cell mate was his head. The head's chin was missing, the upright skull left resting with its top buck teeth against the stone floor. His blonde hair stuck out in blood-covered tufts, his blue eyes wide with shock and terror. A pool of blood had spilled out of the cell and into the corridor.

From the hallway, someone shrieked—breaking my mind from the carnage around me.

A guard ran by the cell, hit the pool of blood, and fell right on his back. He looked over at me and we made eye contact for a brief second. In that contact our eyes said the same thing: *What the fuck is going on?*

A creature crawled up to the guard, moving with an odd kind of grace although it looked like it should be clumsy. It was almost humanoid, naked with pale flesh. It drug deformed legs behind it as it moved, its bald head gleaming in the fluorescent light. One arm seemed useless and thin, while the other was muscled and powerful. It seemed to be smiling and its mouth was full of misshapen and sharp teeth.

The guard shrieked and tried to crawl away through Rabbit's slippery blood. The creature lunged its face forward, pulling a thick chunk of flesh from the man's face like an animal. Blood sprayed so far that I was hit with the droplets standing at least seven feet away.

The creature turned its head toward me and shot me what I took for a grin before it crawled off down the corridor. Off in the distance I could hear more screams, then everything went quiet again.

So now here I stand, alone in my blood-splattered cell. Rabbit's half head stares at me from the floor accusingly. It has been four days now, and no guard has shown his face. I'm convinced that they are all dead. The running water is not working, so I've been forced to drink from the toilet. I'm getting to the point where the fly-covered pieces of Rabbit's flesh are starting to look tasty to me.

How my life had suddenly turned into a surreal nightmare is beyond me. What kind of prison is this place? The creatures seemed to be able to spring right from our dreams? How is it possible? It's baffling.

My plan is to wait one more day, and then I'll be forced to venture into the hole in the ceiling. What will become of me I am quite certain is a death similar to Rabbit's or the guard laying in front of my cell. All I hope is that my death will be as quick as theirs.

I am haunted by these creatures every time I sleep. I am never sure if they are really in the room with me or if it's a dream.

There are times when I wonder if I'm still sleeping as Rabbit watches me, head cocked to the side as he tries to make out what I'm saying. It's amazing to me that I actually wish the annoying prick was back alive. Other times I wonder if it wouldn't be better if I slammed my head into the wall just like Travis did.

I lay back on the bed and close my eyes, awaiting my death. What else can you do when even sleep cannot provide a way of escape?

The last thought that enters my mind before I drift off into my dangerous dreams is of my wasted life and the way I squandered it.

And I wonder if I will wake up in Hell or if I am already there.

ROSAHELLA'S FOOTPRINTS

CARVERTON—1890

Edward came out of his trance to the soft sound of his finger bone scraping against the chiseled letters in his daughter's tombstone. He fell backward onto Rosahella's snow-covered grave, whimpering in disgust, his hand clutched inside the dark folds of his coat. The last few letters of the tombstone were covered with his flesh and blood, a long, snake-like crimson line dripping from the letter A and into the date of her death just below. He held the mangled finger before his face, the white bone peeking from within the milky blood as if behind glass, and wept.

Visitors to Dark Hallow Cemetery were used to the site of the man, clad all in black, kneeling at the graveside of his dead daughter. Not a day passed that Edward Covington did not visit at least once. A common sight would be Edward standing over the grave in the rain; his wiry form as still as the marble angel statues that guarded the entrance of the burial grounds. It was said that he had lost his sanity the day he found his five-year-old daughter dead on the shore of the lake, arms outstretched as if she would take flight, her pale body covered with stab wounds.

Rosahella was not the first child to be found murdered but one of dozens. All of the children were found on the shore of the lake, some of their bodies so small they appeared to be broken dolls. Most of the town children were not allowed to roam the woods outside of town for fear that they would become the next victim.

Edward stood up and stared around the graveyard to see if

he was being watched, holding his hand clenched painfully to his side. Dark Hollow looked strangely beautiful coated with snow, gray tombstones jutting out of an ivory sea. The trees, their leafless branches frosted in white, looked beautiful to his artistic eye. The iron gate that surrounded the cemetery offered a feeling of protection, the spikes encrusted with frost. Dagger-like icicles hung from the roofs of the dozens of mausoleums that lay scattered about, water dropping from the tips and onto the wet ground below.

I wish I could paint it, Edward thought to himself. *Despite all the death here, it is so beautiful.*

Before Rosahella's death, Edward had made his living with nothing more than a paintbrush. He had not painted anything since he lost his daughter. Even the death of his wife a year before Rosahella's had not killed his artistic spirit.

Edward looked down at the grave and tried to imagine his daughter as she had been when alive. The first image that entered his mind was her smile, elegant and exhilarating in its magnificence. When Rosahella smiled, she had the ability to chase away even the worst of moods. The smile was infectious enough, but when followed by the musical sound of her laughter, it was enough to make even the most hardened of men melt. If he closed his eyes, sometimes he could see the way the sunlight glittered off of her golden hair. Feel the way it felt to embrace her when she ran out to meet him when he came home from town.

The soft sound of footsteps approaching in the snow made him open his eyes and he was surprised when he seemed to be alone. He was certain someone had been walking toward him. The sound penetrated the air again, a whispery rustling of movement.

When he saw the imprint of tiny bare feet in the snow just to the left of Rosahella's tombstone, he nearly collapsed. As he watched, the footprints continued to embed themselves into the white ground, stopping only when they came within a few feet of where he stood. Edward forced himself to breathe, but he stood still, knowing with certainty that his dead daughter was standing invisibly before him.

As he watched, words formed in the snow at his feet as by

an imperceptible child's finger. *"Daddy."*

Though Edward struggled to hold in his explosive emotions, a painful sob fired from his mouth in a steamy burst, he fell to his knees before the letters, his finger already tracing the words. It took him a few seconds to realize he was using the exposed bone of his hand and the letters instantly became highlighted with his own crimson blood.

"I miss you, Rosahella," Edward said, his teardrops falling into the snow with a barely audible hiss. "Daddy has never stopped thinking about you."

The footprints moved away a bit and turned around as if they wanted him to follow. Edward stood up and brushed the snow away from his knees. The footprints moved right through the fence of the cemetery and into the dense, snow-covered trees beyond. Trying his best to ignore the pain throbbing in his finger, Edward managed to climb the iron fence, carefully avoiding the sharp spikes by folding his coat.

Rosahella's footprints, patiently waiting as he climbed the fence, started up again once he had crossed. Edward followed his dead daughter silently, both numb and exhilarated at what was happening. He followed the footprints over steep slippery hills, across ice covered streams, through dense foliage and snow covered terrain—ignoring the slicing wind that penetrated deep into his tired bones. Though the snow was deep, Edward sometimes sinking down to his knees, the footprints never went any deeper than an inch.

The trail led Edward to an old gray mansion that rested deep in the ancient forest, a thick wisp of smoke trailing from its brick chimney. The two-story house was kept up well, despite the fact that it was out so far into the woods that visitors were most likely scarce. A wrap around porch, complete with an elaborately carved wooden rail, surrounded the house. The faces of angels, or children, were carved into the wood, all of them gazing toward the heavens with enormous eyes of melancholy. The windows were covered with dark draperies.

Rosahella's footprints walked over to one of the columns that supported the porch and stopped, waiting for Edward to catch up.

Carved expertly into the column of wood, her eyes so vibrant and expressive they appeared alive, was the face of Rosahella.

Edward ran his finger over the wooden nose and lips, a pained moan coming from deep within his throat.

"Can I help you?" a raspy voice asked from behind him. Edward spun around, the words startling after such a long silence.

The man standing behind him had a lengthy dark beard, speckled with generous amounts of gray. A black top hat rested comfortably on his curly hair. His yellow teeth poked out from his stringy lips, giving him the appearance of a rat or some other kind of vermin. The man's eyes were strikingly blue; glowing like newly polished gems. He was unnaturally tall, his spidery legs no thicker than sticks. Crows feet made jagged patterns away from his eyes; the lines only working to emphasize his already striking stare.

"Yes," Edward said, burying his bad hand in his coat. It began to snow, the flakes swirling around their bodies in odd patterns. "Would you mind telling me why the face of my daughter is embedded on the column of your house?"

"Is she?" the man asked. "None of the angels carved into the wood are real. I just carve a face that comes into my mind. If she bears a resemblance to your daughter, maybe it is because she is as beautiful as an angel."

"*Was* beautiful," Edward said, his eyes narrowing.

"Pardon me?"

"Mr..."

"Moore," the man replied. "My name is Jarret Moore."

"Well, my daughter *was* beautiful, Mr. Moore. Rosahella was murdered two years ago."

Moore walked up to the porch and put one black boot upon the step. "I am very sorry to hear that, my good man. I am honored that my angel bears a resemblance to your daughter. It can only mean she is now at one with the denizens of heaven."

Edward nodded and continued to study Moore suspiciously. He thought about pointing out the ghostly footprints that had led him here, but decided against it, instead going with his instincts. Something about the bearded man had a feeling of controlled rage.

Moore looked up at the gray sky and shivered. "Looks like it's going to get worse before it gets better. You can feel it in the air. Would you like to come inside for some tea?"

"I would indeed," Edward replied.

Moore led him inside the immaculately clean house, placing their coats on an oak coat hanger just inside the parlor. More than a half a dozen paintings hung around the hallway, most of them depicting angels in one way or another. An ornate grandfather clock loomed at the end of the hall, the faces of dozens of cherubs peering out somberly from within the reddish wood. The sounds of their boots striking against the hardwood floor resonated through the quiet house as they walked down a dimly-lit hallway. Edward detected a strong scent of flowers, which seemed unusual in the middle of one of the harshest winters on record.

Moore led him to a door just before the massive clock. "This is my study. Go on in. I'll go fetch us some tea."

The study was filled with hundreds of old books, most of them in near perfect condition. A grand table sat in the center, an unlit candelabra in the middle. In one corner of the room sat a small bucket filled to the brim of with the dead petals of flowers, colorful ribbons and bows strewn throughout. A leather-bound copy of John Milton's *Paradise Lost* sat opened on the table, the stem of a dead rose holding the page. Edward placed his finger upon the soft paper and read the first line.

Of Man's first disobedience, and the fruit
Of that forbidden tree whose mortal taste
Brought death into the world, and all our woe.

Edward frowned and turned to the window at his back. Snow was pounding into the glass so fiercely that he could barely see the yard outside. He could not help but feel a little wounded by the fact that Rosahella's footprints would now be completely covered up as if they did not exist.

The sound of a striking match startled Edward from his thoughts and he turned to find Moore lighting the candelabra with a mysterious smile, his long stick-like arm guiding the flame to the wicks. "I thought you might want a little light."

Moore vanished yet again, but returned a few minutes later with two steaming cups of tea. "Sorry for the wait."

Edward nodded and sat down, his body cold and weary from the long trek through the woods. "Thank you, sir."

"It is not a problem at all," Moore said, sitting down. "To be honest, you are the first guest I have received in the last twenty years."

Edward took a sip of the hot tea before speaking. It had a vague taste of apple. "I had no idea I would be venturing into the woods today. To be honest, I was led here."

"Led?" Moore frowned and cocked his head curiously to the side. "Led by whom?"

"My daughter Rosahella."

"But I thought your daughter was—"

"Dead? She is indeed. It's the oddest thing. I followed her ghostly footprints into the snow and I end up here."

"There are other things in these woods than the spirits of dead children," Moore said, sipping repetitively at his tea. "It could have been anything."

"I suppose," Edward replied, carefully studying the man's face. His wounded finger was throbbing painfully in his pocket. "But what kind of spirit would lead me to a life-like wood carving of my dead daughter's face? She led me right from her grave."

Moore started to speak, but closed his mouth and shook his head. Something in the eyes told Edward that the man was disturbed. The strange man stared down into his tea as if he could somehow escape within the cup.

"I found my daughter on the shore of the lake two years ago," Edward whispered, turning to face the howling storm as if he sensed a kindred soul within the ferocious wind. "I was looking for days, but I never stopped, never slept—nothing. She was lying on her back, staring upwards into the sky. Oh God, she looked so peaceful—so beautiful. The lake had washed the blood away and her skin was so white. The way her arms were outstretched, it was as if someone had made a macabre porcelain doll of her. That image has not left my mind for two years. The first picture I conjure up of Rosahella is her dead face. My life has become hell." Edward stopped speaking for a moment, his face reddening as if there was a slow burning fire just behind his moist and haunted eyes. "Rosahella was my life. I was lost when I could not wake up and make her breakfast for school. I was just empty." He choked out the last word and stopped talking again, fighting back his emotions with a pained grimace. "She was my soul. I have not stopped thinking about her for even one moment. I'm dying inside. I don't think I can stop it unless I find out what happened. The bastard stabbed her over thirty times."

"Your daughter is with the angels now," Moore whispered. "That is where all dead children go when they die. Children are not capable of evil. It is what makes them so utterly perfect. What goes wrong that turns men into murderers?"

Edward watched the man speak, his mind exhausted from his own grief. Moore's eyes were filling up with tears as he spoke.

"Something is deeply wrong with a man," Moore continued, his voice taking on a resigned tone as he stood up. "A man who gives into his temptations. When a child dies it is as if the world stops. It wounds us all. I wish I could just cease."

"You sound as if you are responsible," Edward said.

Moore paused for a moment, something dark stirring from deep within his face. He moaned and an anguished sound fell from his quivering mouth. It was as if he was trying to hold a tremendous weight and was only moments from being crushed to death. Something *snapped* behind his cryptic eyes and his body sagged momentarily, a wheezing sigh nearly pulling him to his knees. Moore picked up the bucket of dead flowers from the corner of the room and set it gently upon the table. "You must only take what belongs to you."

Edward stood up and peered into the bucket, his good hand shaking as he plunged it within the decaying petals. The realization that the numerous colorful bows and ribbons belonged to the murdered children struck him like a blow and he nearly collapsed into the chair just as his finger closed over the bracelet.

Edward pulled the bracelet from the bucket, watching the dead petals fall from the gold as if in slow motion. The initials of Rosahella Covington could clearly be seen carved into the side.

"I'm so sorry," Moore whispered, wincing as if he was in agony. The wind bellowed outside of the window directly behind him. His gaunt silhouette stood out in dark contrast to the swirling snow at his back. He let his head drop toward the floor, though his eyes still stayed in contact with the father he had broken.

Edward gripped the bracelet so fiercely that it broke his skin, holding it up toward the ceiling. Blood ran down the gold and onto the pale flesh of his wrist. He closed his eyes tightly, clenching his jaw as if someone had just slipped a knife into the small of his back. "Tell me," he hissed, tears falling from his closed eyes. "Tell me why. You have destroyed me—the very least you could do is tell me this."

"She was walking in the woods," Moore said, his words soft. "I could not stop myself. I have never been able to stop once I see them. See the angels. Children often use the woods for shortcuts. She smiled when I approached her and offered me a piece of her candy. I returned her smile and placed the candy upon my tongue. She was too beautiful to be of this world. She belonged in heaven. I took my knife from the sheath at my side and plunged it into her stomach. I can still see her eyes as she died—so exquisite. So lost was I that I did not realize how many times the knife broke her flesh. I took her to the lake and placed her within the water. I regret murdering her. I regret murdering them all. I cannot stop."

The two men scrutinized one another in the candlelight— the shrieking wind the only sound. Edward looked like a man too tired to live; his mouth hung slack, his ebony eyes nothing more than burned holes within his flesh.

"Help me," Moore said, placing a dagger on the table before the candelabra. "Stop me from doing it again."

Edward placed his hand upon the hilt of the blade, soft air hissing from his mouth. "You are a monster."

Moore swallowed deeply, a strange half smile on his face, eyes closed. "I know."

Edward plunged the knife into Moore's chest, the hot blood splattering into his face in a sanguinary mist.

Moore exhaled, a wet sound that was more of a sigh than a cry of pain. He opened his eyes and stared into Edward's, a curiously peaceful smile on his angular face. Edward met his gaze, feeling the thumping of the murderer's heartbeat reverberating through the dagger and into the bones of his fingers. When Moore's heart finally stopped, Edward let him fall to the floor. The wind and snow outside had suddenly stopped and the unexpected quiet gave his tired mind a feeling of clarity.

Edward picked up the candelabra and held the flames to Moore's clothing. The fire was gradual at first, but soon had enveloped the child murderer, the crackling of his skin breaking the silence of the house. The smell of burning flesh stabbed into his nostrils and he stopped breathing momentarily to chase away the nausea.

He set afire *Paradise Lost* and let it burn for a few seconds before using it to ignite some of the other books. When Edward finally walked out of the library, his eyes dazed and tired, the room was nearly consumed by flames

Edward stood outside in the frigid cold and watched his fire devour Jarret Moore's mansion, his face stoic. "For Rosahella," he began to chant like a mantra, watching the flames flicker and dance demonically from the windows. The elaborately carved columns burned brighter than the rest of the house, flames licking from within the wide eyes of the children.

Edward waited until the house collapsed, the black smoke drifting up toward the gray sky as if offering the children's souls to heaven.

Though he was tired, Edward made his way back through the snow-covered wilderness and Dark Hollow. An hour later, he found himself standing once again before Rosahella's grave, clutching his now unbearably painful hand within his singed coat. The sun was setting behind his back and the sky above was pink, giving the cemetery an unusual, yet beautiful glow.

"The monster is dead, Rosahella," Edward whispered, brushing snow away from the tombstone before placing the bloody bracelet atop of it. "So many of you suffered."

The breeze was light at first, the edges of Edward's long coat flickering around his legs softly. Moments later, a gust of icy wind blasted into his body, nearly pushing him backwards. The whispers of dozens of children caressed his ears, as if they were somehow drifting within the wind itself.

The scent of fresh flowers filled his nostrils and his eyes widened.

Edward waited, sensing something monumental in the icy air he breathed, biting his bottom lip as if he was about to be taken down by a violent blow.

A deep imprint suddenly appeared in the snow in front of the grave—the body of a small child. It was as if an invisible child had dropped from the rose-colored sky above. The outline of angel's wings sprung out from the side of the imprint, a perfect snow angel.

The wind detonated through Dark Hallow, the air coming alive with ghostly laughter. Dozens of snow angels sprung up around him, the sounds of tiny arms brushing against snow entering his ears. Ice crystals brushed his grinning face as they were picked up by the swirling wind. Snow began to fall in heavy flakes, twisting and whirling around Edward's body as if alive. Columns of snow spun and danced around him like translucent wraiths, rainbows forming in the dawn sunlight.

Edward looked to the sky above and began to weep, spinning around in the snow amongst all of the angels, arms raised into the air, his laughter carrying through the cemetery air like a bittersweet song.

SOME OF US ARE LOOKING AT THE STARS

"It looks peaceful enough," Baker said, his eyes calmly scanning Outpost 727, the largest space station ever built by the Dark Alliance.

I nodded before looking back at the pilot, letting my fingers run through my white hair. It had gone from dark to white seemingly overnight during the war. "It does, doesn't it? Seeing it that peaceful just makes me all the more nervous. I feel like a small animal sneaking down to the river to take a drink where the lion's live."

"I still can't believe they are just sending one man and not a fucking army," Baker said, removing his gaze from the screen and looking me over. His face registered that he was unimpressed with my rather unthreatening appearance. "Sydney Vale has a very deadly reputation."

I smiled and looked back toward the hulking space station. It rested ungracefully amongst the beautiful stars, turning clumsily in the silence of space. A few of the portholes were glowing with some odd, reddish cast. "Well, it's certainly not because of my prowess in combat. I'm just a pilot. Syd and I go back a long way. We grew up together. We also shared a mutual friend. Paris was killed in the war, though."

"Vale murdered Senator Huxley last month when he tried to check up on him. Sent some video feed of Huxley's severed head with electrical-like wires stuck into it. He also killed twenty or so soldiers, guards and aides." Baker grinned at me, his smile flashing from his thick beard. "I don't know about you, but that would bother the hell out of me. Not only that, he has a little private army in there."

"That he does," I said, watching as our small space ship came into docking distance.

"Well, you still haven't explained why they aren't sending an army."

I was already walking toward the door when I heard his comment, and I turned around to face him, my voice soft. "If you were the Dark Alliance and you had already lost a very important political Senator, would you send an army or a former friend."

"I would send the army. Wipe his ass out. We'd probably get some casualties, but at least the risk would be gone. Why would they send you, you ain't but a man?"

"Because, I'm expendable," I said, leaving the room to his soft chuckling.

I studied my haggard face in the mirror, trying to prepare myself mentally to go into Outpost 727. Sydney Vale's dark eyes swam into my mind, and I wondered what he would do.

The last time I saw him was at least ten years ago. We met on Krassnar 3, a neutral space station situated between the two higher powers. It was just after the Virus wars, and the Dark Alliance had been victorious.

When I met Sydney Vale at the bar that night, neither of us were smiling. We had lost too many friends in the war to feel any true sense of satisfaction. As far as I'm concerned, Victory only feels good when it's glamorized in movies and novels. When you have lost as many close friends and family members as I have to the war, victory feels just as fucking bitter as defeat. Celebrating is like throwing a party in a room full of the corpses of your friends. It just feels wrong.

"I can't help but feel tortured at the fact that Paris is not here with us," I said, taking a long sip of my drink.

His eyes flashed then, and I got the kind of feeling that one gets when you are about to see extreme aggression. It almost appeared as if Syd was struggling to hold back a door, that if opened, would blow up the whole station. His face was entirely calm. I saw all this in his raging eyes. Syd's voice was low. "Paris did not deserve to die like that. Would you believe he lasted five hours under the Reaper?"

The Reaper was a device that could only be described as an electrified razor blade. It both cut and burned the flesh, finding nerve endings with the precision of a surgeon. It could even remove eyelids without damaging the eyes.

"No, I didn't know that. Perhaps now isn't the time to discuss this, Syd. I kind of want to relax tonight. Lord knows we deserve it."

"I don't know if I'm going to stay with the Alliance," Sydney said, sipping slowly from his glass. "Every time I look into space it reminds me of what I've lost. I think I need to get down on a planet."

I chuckled. "You wouldn't know what to do with yourself on a planet, Syd. You'd go fucking crazy."

Syd smiled then, and I swear there hasn't been a sleepless night where I didn't see that eerie smile in my dreams. It was a sharp smile, the kind that seemed to stab into your face with the apathetic violence of a sharp blade. His eyes glittered like icy stars in the dim lighting of the bar and I felt myself actually wince. At that moment, I knew how much Syd had lost and it wasn't just friends.

It was his fucking mind.

He stared at me with those razor eyes, and that smile, and said, "I'm already fucking crazy, Randall. I don't give a shit about anything anymore. When you get to where I'm at, nothing matters but the memories." He started to laugh then, a chilly, almost computer-like titter that sounded nothing like the warm man I grew up with.

I didn't return his laughter, only offered a fake smile and nodded. Syd threw his money on the table and got up. "I'm truly going to miss you, my friend. Our paths better cross again."

As I watched him go, his back rigid from years of military training, I realized the sad truth. Sydney Vale, even though he was walking away from me, was already amongst my dead friends.

The doors hissed closed behind me as I entered the docking bay. For a brief moment, I thought Syd wasn't going to let me in. Some part of me didn't want to go in. It was my orders that if I thought things weren't going well then I was to kill him. Whether or not I would be able to go through with the murder of a good friend was a debate I didn't want to torture myself with right now.

I stared at the doors, waiting patiently, my fists clenched at my sides. The only sound in the bay was my own soft breathing and a strange, dull roar beyond the entrance to Outpost 727. I felt something soft brush the back of my neck, almost as if someone had dragged a piece of thread across it.

I knew at that moment that Syd was watching me from the security camera, knowing how impatient I was and probably a little amused. I kept my body language still, not allowing him the pleasure of knowing how annoyed I was.

"I really missed you, Randall," a voice said from the speaker just above the door. It sounded machine-like and lifeless, but something in the inflection stabbed into my psyche like a blistering needle of recognition. "You have no idea how good it is to see your face."

Before I could complete my thought, the double doors whispered open in front of me. I flinched visibly, stepping backwards when the music blasted into the previously quiet docking bay. It was a classical piece by one of my favorites, Gregor Handel, a composer that both Syd and I loved. I inhaled deeply before stepping into the dimly lit corridor, my mind resigned to the blunt fact that whether I accomplished my goal or not, I would be betraying my friend.

There was a man standing in the corridor as I entered, his body so still that for a brief moment I thought he was a mannequin. He wore a black military-like uniform, a stark contrast to the light blue and white colors I was used to seeing as a member of the Alliance. His head turned slightly, and our eyes made contact. He had no whites in his eyes, only an ebony sea of moisture, dull red pupils in the middle like a droplet of blood. The crow's feet around his eyes were tightly etched into his unusually smooth white flesh, snaking across his temples like tribal tattoos. He nodded then—his pale chin coming down so slow I was reminded of a reptile, his closely cropped hair gleaming in the fluorescent lighting. Then, with a slow movement of his hand, indicated that I follow the corridor. I was surprised that he had not asked me to relinquish any weapons, but I certainly wasn't going to remind him of it.

The music continued to play as we walked, seeming to fit right perfectly in the militaristic design of the station, all order and mathematical perfection. I could feel the sweat dripping from the pits of my arms, falling to my side like blood from cold wounds.

We stopped at the doors of an elevator and my escort kept back, watching me clinically with his hands behind him. There was something inhuman about him, something almost alien. He stood there watching me, his body impossibly still, studying me with that unnerving gaze. Shivering, I turned to face the elevator, feeling his stare on my back like the touch of murderer's fingertip.

I concentrated on the digital numbers above the door, imagining them to be the countdown to a bomb. The humming of the elevator could barely be heard over the music and I resisted an urge to turn around to face my guard. I imagined that he was only inches behind me, studying me with his dead eyes, his teeth bared to bite hungrily into the back of my neck.

I stopped breathing when the doors opened, my knees quivering underneath my wiry frame, my hands curling up into tight little balls. My breath shot out in a hiss of air, my mouth immediately firing sharp staccato wisps of my own shock. "Paris," I found myself whispering, my voice sounding ghostly in the now quiet corridor.

My dead friend stood there, an out of place grin under his dark eyes, his chalky hand held out to me. His head was shaven—long black veins winding around his skull like spidery shatter lines on broken glass. A large indented area stood out on his forehead, about the size of an apple, and it took me a moment to realize that it was a closed, third eye. I took his outstretched arm by instinct, his cold fingers enveloping my warm hand.

He pulled me to him then, his rancid breath shooting into my face, squeezing me in a frigid embrace. "I knew you would come, Randall," he whispered into my ear. "We all knew you would come. God, it's good to see you again."

I was numb, but I heard myself say, "My god, Paris, you're dead."

"Not anymore, Randall," he said, pulling me tighter into his arms. "Not anymore."

"But they took your DNA from the lab. The Reaper—"

He laughed then, the sound of wings fluttering, his third eye opening. It was entirely red—looking more like an almond shaped bullet hole than an eye. "I crossed back. You have no idea the beautiful things I have seen."

I felt the elevator rising, pulling me upward with the disconcerting feeling that he was soaring with me in his frosty arms.

"You'll see too, Randall," he added. I saw what appeared to be tiny fingers dragging across the red sheen that was his third eye. My stomach felt the punch when I realized it was some sort of spider. I could see dozens of them swimming around through the red window into his head.

"Hello, my friend," Sydney Vale purred behind me, his voice taking on a liquid inflection.

He was standing with his back to the viewing window, the stars winking around his gaunt form and shaven head, his face turned to the side like crescent moon in the darkness. His arms were held rigidly to his sides, reminding me momentarily of the ancient film *Nosferatu*. His third eye glowed silently from the center of his head, a reddish tinge highlighting his arched eyebrows. He was grinning, his dark mouth a black slit on his snowy face.

To his right was a machine that could only be described as organic. Thousands of wires shot out from a pulsating red globe, piercing into the severed heads of Alliance soldiers that circled around it like some perverse sculpture, their mouths slowly grinding together like they were chewing. One of them was Senator Huxley. All their eyes were turned toward me, seeming to plead to be destroyed. Above the globe was some sort of scaly insect, its thick, tentacles seeming to undulate like it was breathing, or sucking the life of the soldiers.

Syd walked toward me then, moving so gracefully that he seemed to float, his palms outstretched in what seemed to be a mockery of a crucifixion. "I would love to hear what they are saying about me, Randall. Old Sydney Vale's gone fucking insane right? Send his old friend to talk some sense into him? Kill him if that fails?"

He stopped when he was only inches from my face, the red window in his forehead glowing like a perverse beacon in the gloomy light. Small, parasitic tick-like insects could be seen swimming around inside, their legs dragging across the surface, some of them even penetrating outside.

His thin lips pulled back, exposing his metallic teeth. His mouth was red. "I'm not insane. Would you bring back your dead friends if you could, Randall? You know you would."

"I would never try and kill you, Syd," I found my deadened voice saying. "I love you like a brother."

Syd stopped smiling, dark shadows slithering across his smooth scalp as he moved. I noticed then that they weren't crow's feet around the eyes after all, but the raven tentacles of some sort of creature embedded deeply into the flesh of his temples. "I know." He gestured toward the organic machine. "I found Them you know, or They found me. I think they sensed my loathing toward the Gods, Randall. They sensed I wanted to strike back."

He held out his wrists, and I could see his veins as if they were made of glass. Tiny spiders could be seen in them. "They entered my body near the end of the war, most likely when I lay rotting in that cell on Tanex Five. The change was quick. I took this job as Commander of this station knowing I had some purpose. We're all here now, Paris and Joseph. Even Gordon is here." He gave me what he probably thought was a warm smile, but it only came out as creepy. "You can even bring back your mother if you want."

Gordon was a childhood friend that had drowned when we were back in high school on earth. I was often haunted by memories of those days. When I realized I would be overjoyed to see Gordon again, I froze, the realization that I was being drawn into Syd's world and its corruption seeping into my flesh like poison.

"Syd you aren't even certain what you're doing here," I said, a sudden insight detonating in my mind. "You don't know that's its really even them. They could be fucking byproducts of your own damn memory of them for all you know."

"You say that because you cannot see, Randall. I promise you that you will see differently by tomorrow."

I turned toward Paris. "Do you remember what we talked about the night before you left for the war?"

Paris nodded, that fake smile on his face. "Of course I do."

I waited in silence and when he didn't say anything, I spoke again. "Well, tell me, Paris. What were the last words you told me?"

"God, I don't remember, Randall," he said robotically, a parody of his former self. "That was years ago."

"Let me give you a hint. You were looking out the window, and you told me it was your favorite aphorism. You told me that you would never quote it to Syd, saying that he would not understand."

Syd moved stepped up to me, his inky eyes widening in rage. "Leave him the fuck alone."

"He doesn't know because it's not him, Syd. All these people are just creations of your own mind and those fucking aliens you have wired into your whacked out brain."

"Shut up," he hissed, his voice taking on a dangerous edge.

"But, Syd, he would know. He has it tattooed on the center of his back. That's how important it was to him. It said, 'We're all sitting in the gutter, but some of us are looking at the stars'."

"I said shut the fuck up!" He howled, spinning me around and hurling me into the view screen. I hit the glass hard, my breath shooting out of my lungs like the firing of a gun.

He was on me then, a pearl handled straight razor in his hand, a blade he had carried with him since we were kids. "I will send you to the other side," he said, the spiders stuck to the eye in his forehead obscenely. His rotting breath shot into my face, entering my nostrils like a physical entity.

I felt the blade slicing painfully into the skin of my neck. "It won't be me," I wheezed. "Just a half assed mirror image of your decaying mind. You aren't raising the dead, Syd, only your memories. You aren't striking back at God."

"You'll understand, Randall," he said, a golden teardrop falling down his cheek. "You'll understand when I bring you back."

I actually heard the ripping sound of my own throat, saw my crimson blood splattering into his snow-white face. I fell backwards and stared through the glass into space. I knew I wasn't coming back. Oddly, I didn't care that I was dying.

I stared into Sydney Vale's black eyes, noticing a glimmer of light in their murky depths, a dim shimmering over the blackness. He squeezed my arm, a final gesture before I went to the other side.

I turn away from a friend I once loved and look through the window.

Stars twinkle in my dying eyes, oscillate to the shallow beating of my heart as blood soaks my shirt. Remembering all I have lost, countless friends who died for nothing, I notice Syd's moon-like face reflected on the glass, a dim milky gleam on an endless black canvas. The glowing red eye in the center of his head throbs like a heart among the stars.

I look past his reflection—Syd's sharp breathing the only sound—and let my gaze drift into the immense darkness of space.

THE DARK REALITY OF BANNEN WILDE

"I can see into your mind," the oily man said, his dark eyes narrowing into glassy points. He leaned back and studied her expression, a shy smile on his face.

Amy turned away just as his scent hit her nostrils—a combination of dead flowers and sweat. "I think you have the wrong person."

She knew how dangerous it would be to take the subway this time of night, but she had little choice. Her funds had been scarce as of late, forcing her to sell the car. Life had been hellish since her husband had been murdered mysteriously outside their apartment. Now, she was sitting here in the nearly empty subway car with this psychotic, nothing but a sleeping passenger to prevent any violence he might do against her. She thought of how good a warm bath and the classical music of Handel would make her feel and hoped the man would go away.

The strange man did not answer her statement at first. Instead he just stared at her, smile widening, red lips stretching over his misshapen teeth. His white face was unnaturally smooth, marked only by two long scars that snaked from his fiery eyes to his chin, offering the illusion his teardrops had been made of acid and had burned roads into the flesh. Stringy black hair fell from his pale head like greasy, ebony ropes and his ears jutted out from his skull. His massive height gave him a freakish appearance. Tight black clothing encased his wiry frame, arms extending from his body in stick-like branches. A dark trench coat waved around him like a dream, undulating softly to its own hidden wind. He wiggled his serpent-like fingers back and forth, tongue darting out, licking his thin lips sensually.

"I, too, like the music of Handel," the man purred. His voice had a liquid inflection to it, each word having a singsong quality. "It makes me feel so…divine, as if I can reach my hand out and touch heaven for the briefest of moments. There are not a lot of things out there that can make one feel like that, Amy."

She froze, her hands digging into her purse as she tried to remember if she had spoken her thoughts aloud. When Amy realized she found the man arousing, she wanted to run.

"Weren't you listening to me, Amy," he said, moving forward, his voice reverberating around the car. "I told you I can see into your mind. Do you think I'm a madman? Not many have lived long after thinking Bannen Wilde was a madman."

Amy swallowed, uncomfortable at how small the subway car suddenly seemed.

"It doesn't suddenly seem small. These cars are not very big. Why?" He leaned in closer, head cocking to the side as he grinned, ebony pupils pulsing to the beat of his heart. His teeth were irregularly long and white and she could smell his cloying candy-tainted breath. "It's okay to be afraid, you know. Fear helps some people stay alive. It's an instinct far too many ignore."

He looked up and closed his eyes. Amy could see his eyeballs moving from behind his lids like a sleeper lost in his own erotic dreams.

"God gave you that sense to protect you when you are in danger," he continued, his voice soothing.

Wilde's eyes fluttered open with sound of butterfly wings and he stared down at her, grinding his crooked teeth before he spoke. "You should listen to that fear, Amy. It saves wild animals from a certain death."

"What the hell are you?" Amy asked, wishing the sleeping passenger at the end of the car would wake up.

"Oh, he's not sleeping," Wilde said. He walked to the end of the car and lifted up the head, exposing gaping eye sockets before letting the victim fall forward and onto the floor.

Amy shrieked and ran toward the back of the car.

"I wouldn't go in there if I were you!" he shouted. "The world is a different place there!"

She pulled at the door, hurling herself forward into the car ahead.

The first impression she got as she stepped into the next car was she was looking at an incredibly life-like painting. Frozen passengers surrounded her, the bodies as still as stone. The beat of the train going over the tracks was the only sound.

The inside of the train had an ornate, almost Victorian appearance. The lighting was dim, giving an eerie cast to the faces of the motionless passengers. For a brief moment, she was so stunned by what she was seeing she almost forgot about her pursuer. Exhaling sharply, she whipped around to face him, her throat ready to fire a scream into the silent car.

She looked through a window. The railroad tracks faded into the darkness as they were devoured by the night. Large, twisted trees walled the track, offering the illusion they were hurling through an eerie, nightmare induced-tunnel.

Amy turned around to face the ghostly passengers, biting her lip to prevent herself from sobbing aloud.

Oh my god, oh my god, oh my god, she chanted in her mind like a mantra, staring at the passengers with wide eyes.

One passenger in particular caught her attention, and she crept forward to get a better look.

His clear blue eyes looked through her, the eyes of a doll. He had a teacup to his open mouth. A thick mustache drooped over his upper lip and his tongue protruded out. His hair was oiled and parted in the middle, an older style. His face appeared hard, as if it was made of wax.

Amy put her finger in the cup to feel if the tea was solid. Her finger touched a hard surface, the tea as stiff as its unfortunate passenger. She put her finger out tentatively and touched the man's cheek.

The man's blue eyes flicked up at her, stared at her for a few penetrating seconds, and immediately darted back down at the teacup.

Amy fell backwards and stared around at the passengers as if they would soon detonate into life. Standing up slowly, as if moving too fast would bring them upon her, she studied her surroundings for a possible way out.

To her right was a beautiful woman, mouth opened in silent laughter. In the seat next to her, a little girl was frozen in mid-speech. The scene gave her the impression the child had said something the woman had found funny.

Some passengers stared out of the dark windows, watching the trees fly by perpetually. Others slept, their bodies so still they appeared to be corpses.

A soft titter interrupted the silence and Amy stood rigid, staring around the room in a panicked effort to find the source.

She knew it was from the man in the last car. What did he say his name was? *Bannen, Bannen Wilde,* she thought. Just saying his name made her tingle in ways that terrified, giving her the impression she was being charmed by a monster that would consume her flesh.

She turned toward each passenger with a corrupting feel of dread, her legs shaking. The woman who was frozen in mid-laughter was looking at her now. Was she doing that before?

The little girl began to nod, the rest of her body as still as a photograph. "I told you not to come in here, Amy," she said with Wilde's voice, eyes glowing in the gloomy lighting of the train car.

The rest of the passengers began to emit wet ripping noises, almost if their organs were being torn apart from the inside. Their flesh undulated—the skin on the face appearing to breathe as it rose gently up and down.

The laughing woman's throat swelled, stretching forward tautly as the skin convulsed. Her head fell back before exploding open in a discharge of spiders—thousands of them spewing forth like vomit. The sounds of tearing flesh filled the train car. The other passengers fell apart, spiders jumping from their mutilated corpses and onto the carpeted floor.

Screaming, her vocal cords almost snapping from the strain, Amy fled.

The next car was similar to the first, its modern feel quite apparent by the up to date advertisements that dotted the surrounding walls. The lights of the tunnel flashed across the window, giving a disconcerting strobe effect.

Bannen Wilde was standing at the end of the car, arms

stretched out in an obscene crucifixion pose. His elongated head was down toward the floor and he looked up, a menacing smile flaring up underneath his fierce eyes, his rope-like hair flowing to a phantom wind.

"Yes, Amy. I am real," he said, his voice a lecherous purr. Bringing his arms down to his side like the beginnings of a mysterious dance, he widened his smile.

Amy felt her sanity pouring away. When she heard the strange giggling, she was astonished to find out it was her own. Part of her knew she was being seduced somehow, but she no longer felt fear. "What do you want?" she asked, surprised at how little she cared at what would happen to her.

"I want to corrupt you, Amy," Wilde said, moving forward elegantly, his hips swaying like a dancer. "I want you to stay in my world."

"I don't understand," Amy said, her brain shrieking as she realized she wanted to embrace him. "You're doing something to me. I find you repulsive."

"You are drawn to me, Amy," he whispered, stepping so close he was only inches away. He leaned forward, smelling her neck, letting his nose drag across her flesh as his hot breath entered her ear like a soothing drug. "Is that so hard to understand? Didn't you ever feel you had a soul mate? I can give you everything. There is nothing I cannot manipulate. Nothing can touch me. And if you stay with me, Amy, nothing will touch *us*. We will have eternity to share and the threads of reality will be ours to cut or tie as we so choose."

Her breath came out in whispers of air, her skin trembling. She was stunned at how badly she wanted him to touch her. "Please, let me go."

"I've been watching you for a long time," he said, kissing her ear, sliding his hot tongue across the lobe. "I want you to join me, Amy. I want you with me. I exist outside of reality, outside of time. Would you not want to live in that kind of world? A world where you cannot age or be harmed by physical objects? A world where you can be as powerful as you want to be? There are no limits, Amy. None."

By this point, she was lost. Although Amy knew she was

being mesmerized by the man who stood before her, she did not care.

The subway car stopped, and a young man entered, walkman headphones surrounding his head. The man's blond hair was cut short, and he was wearing a black concert t-shirt. He seemed oblivious to Amy and Wilde's presence, walking right by them like they did not exist. An elderly man in a fedora and an old ratty suit also entered the car, sat down, and buried his head in a newspaper.

"They can't see us," Wilde said, reading her thoughts as he ran his slender fingers through her dark hair. "That's the beauty of where I exist. No one can see us. We can watch anything we want. The private most soul-searching moments are ours to view. We are not even limited to this time frame, history is ours to view or manipulate. Have you ever felt you had done something before? Walked into a room and felt it was different somehow? That means a Manipulator reshaped your reality. That's what I do, Amy. I manipulate reality. You can do that, too."

Amy shivered and leaned back, enjoying the way his touch felt, like an acid tinged razor upon her flesh. Wilde kissed her, darting his tongue into her mouth, filling it with his oddly sweet taste. She kissed him back, running her hands over his protruding ribs, enjoying the way his hard bones felt underneath his clothing. Some part of her mind remembered what she used to be, but she felt Bannen Wilde inside her, pushing her thoughts away.

"I want you to see what I see, Amy. When we are done, you will be able to read my thoughts as easily as I can yours. I have been lonely, so lonely. I want someone to share eternity with."

She removed her dress, letting it fall to her ankles.

Wilde let his sharp nails penetrate her pantyhose, tearing the material away like flesh, running his long fingers through her pubic hair. The subway car lurched forward as he entered Amy—the floor vibrating underneath them as they hurled into the tunnel.

Black tears were streaming down the sides of Amy's face—her eyes clenched tightly shut, teeth biting into her lip so hard she began to bleed down the sides of her face. She began to sense Wilde's thoughts as he rammed himself into her—his fingers entrenched deeply into her hair. Those thoughts made her giddy, each one offering her more power than the next.

The man with the walkman was nodding his head to his music, unaware of what was going on only feet away. The old man continued to read, his lips moving softly.

Amy was screaming when he came, feeling the last bit of herself die inside her mind. It was like a rebirth. Her flesh had lost all color, and was now as white as Wilde's.

Wilde pulled out of her, a ghostly smile on his bone-white face. His eyes danced joyously in their sockets. "You are mine."

Amy smiled back, taking Wilde's hand in hers. She studied her white flesh, marveling at how silky it looked. Gazing around, she was awed at her ability to see everything. Not just details of the car but everything immediately beyond.

She could feel the touch of every lover, caressing her skin in ways she did not realize was possible. The knife of every murderer entered her body as she stared into the multiple threads of reality, cutting deep into her flesh, twisting in. She saw every possibility and she closed her eyes and moaned, overwhelmed by such power, yet hungry for it.

She was able to see Bannen's thoughts now, and they excited her. The world they existed in was outside of her normal reality. Even time was nothing to her now, it was like she had been living on a single thread, only to see there were millions of others once she was given the ability to perceive them. He thought of himself as a Manipulator, a predator who had worlds of bodies to play with.

"And you are mine," she said, finally noticing her own body at the other end of the car. It looked like she was sleeping, her head back, eyes closed.

"That is but a shell," Wilde purred. "You are in my world now."

"Our world," she corrected him, her voice an exhilarated whisper. For a brief moment, she grieved for what she once was, but the thought left her as quickly as it came. Smiling, she turned to face her lover. "I'm hungry."

Wilde laughed, staring down at the old man, his head turning to the side like an animal studying prey. Reaching out his hand, his fingers wiggling in strange patterns, he sliced a wound across the man's throat. Blood sprayed into the air, splattering Wilde's pale face in crimson droplets.

Amy grinned and launched herself onto the victim, her now-sharp teeth gnashing into his skull. She did not even think it odd when she swallowed his ear, crunching the cartilage between her teeth.

The old man screamed as they fed, his body undulating back and forth to what seemed like invisible puppet strings. Deep wounds opened up on his face as flesh disappeared in fountains of blood.

When they were done feeding, Amy leaned over and kissed Wilde, sharing the old man's blood with the writhing of their tongues. As they tasted each other, the old man continued to shriek, filling the car with obscene background music.

Wilde pulled away, his face splattered with the blood of their victim, eyes glowing on his scarlet face. "This is only the beginning, my love," he said.

They kissed again, rolling around on the mutilated flesh of their victim, enjoying the sound of the old man's screams in the closed confine of the subway car.

STANDING BETWIXT WORLDS IN DELIGHTFUL AGONY

I started hurting myself as a way to deal with stress. During one particularly brutal week in graduate school, I began to cut myself with a razor blade. After an hour of carving thin red lines into my chest, I could not believe how good I felt. It was as if every problem that had ever bothered me had been torn away from my psyche, followed by an adrenaline rush of pure joy. Watching, as the razor sliced so cleanly into my soft flesh, was exhilarating. The way that the blood would bead up behind the blade made me feel like a talented painter, my body being the macabre canvas. Somehow it gave me the feeling of control that I so desperately needed.

It was that simple.

From that point on, I spiraled downward. I could not turn back.

I lost my fiancé later that semester. The way her eyes widened the first time she stuck her hand underneath my shirt to caress me and felt the jagged scars and drying scabs was both sad and comical at the same time. I could tell by the way that she gawked at me as I explained myself that she felt that I had gone mad. Although her face still dances painfully across my mind in the darkest hours of the night, I know that I am better off without her. Losing her only pushed me further into my world of self-mutilation.

As the year went on, every time I felt like I was about to lose control of my life, I would mutilate my body. As I study myself in the mirror, my fingers tracing over the hundreds of crisscrossing scar lines and fresh wounds, I smile and cock my head. It's almost impossible to remember the college student that

I once was, but if I try, I can almost see my formerly handsome face.

Many people would accuse me of being a sick freak, but they just don't understand. To experience pain makes you more human. It lets you understand the human condition in ways that the normal person cannot do. It almost becomes like an exploration of the mind and soul, your body becoming the ultimate teacher. When I am mutilating myself, I get to journey to the furthest level of my psyche. After any particularly ferocious mutilation, I am often hit with an overwhelming and profound feeling of joy.

I had no idea that by exploring the limits of the human body, that I would bypass the line of reality and see beyond.

The pain began to creep insidiously into my sex life, taking me to yet another level of control. In fact, it soon became the only way that I was able to arouse myself. This divine agony allows me to give in to the desires that many people have not yet discovered. Pleasuring myself to my own slippery blood has given me orgasms that can only be described as spiritual. During a moment of intense pain, I feel so alive that I can almost weep.

I can no longer grow any hair on my body. I long ago burned any flesh away that would enable me to do so. My upper lip is missing, giving me a sort of permanent and ghoulish smile. I have to put constant drops of moisture into my left eye, as I have no eyelid. So that the eye will not dry out when I sleep, I am forced to place wet towels over my face. I have no toes on my feet, and I am also missing all the fingers on my right hand. My entire left ear is missing, as well as half of my right one. Most of my body is a mass of red and pink scar tissue.

As you can tell? by that description, I have the type of appearance that would make small children flee in terror.

Last week, my ex-fiancé called me up to see how I was doing. Hearing her voice for the first time in many months brought so many phantom memories up from my past that it overwhelmed me. For the briefest of moments, I felt like the old Will Parker—the one who was capable of loving without pain. A quick look into the mirror abruptly detonated those memories.

I was actually crying as I hung up the phone. It was painful to realize that some part of me wanted to retreat back to my former self. Once you have reached the point that I have, there is no way to turn around.

I can tell by this point that I have lost you. You have already judged me as a pathetic man in profound need of help. What most people do not realize is that I am holding closed the door to all that is harmful in the universe. Once I let go of this door, or if I no longer have the strength to hold it closed, then it will explode open, sending violent chaos upon you.

Riley started helping me about two years ago. It became impossible to mutilate myself in the ways that I wanted. It got to a point that I would fall into unconsciousness just as I was beginning to see the Watchers. Although I know that Riley is a sick man, and gets off sexually when he mutilates me, I care deeply for him. Like me, he is a soldier in the battle against the violators of our world—against the Watchers. Together we try to learn more about why they are visiting us. We hope that once we learn enough, we will be able to destroy them.

I have a theory. It came to me one night as I ran my hands tenderly over glistening wounds that I could no longer feel. The pain that I had at first fallen in love with had almost become unattainable. Lately, it has been more difficult for me to see the Watchers. I am no longer able to feel the pain at the level of intensity that is necessary to view them, and thus, I have been blinded. My theory is that there is a way that I may be able to permanently see the Watchers. A way that if I survive will enable us to take this fight to its bitter and brutal end.

Riley pulled his dirty white t-shirt down over his protruding belly. "Are you sure that this won't kill you, Will?"

"No. I am not sure," I said as I lay back on the table. "But do we really have a choice? It's getting harder for me to see them."

Riley pulled the trigger on the drill and the bit twirled around with a steady hum. I could tell that he was excited by the way that his tongue ran lecherously around his thick lips. "Are you ready?"

I placed the stick in my mouth and said through my teeth, "Yes."

Riley stuck the drill on the side of my head just above where my left ear used to be.

"Remember, as soon as you feel it puncture through my skull you need to stop. If you put that thing directly into my brain, it will be over for me."

Riley nodded and gently pushed his finger on the trigger. At first I felt no pain at all, the nerves on my skin had long since died. When the drill bit began to dig deeper into my flesh, the pain was explosive. My skull shook and vibrated underneath my skin as the bit stabbed, jarring my teeth brutally, spittle flying my wailing mouth in thick streams. I could see my blood splattering onto the floor and onto Riley's tan loafers. I began to moan in pleasure—feeling so elevated that I felt that I could touch God. It felt as if my whole body had become a sexual instrument, my blood squirting out of my wounds like an intense orgasm.

"Go slower," I hissed through gritted teeth. "You're almost through the skull." I could feel myself close to passing out, and I fought the urge with all my energy.

There was a soft *pop* as the bit penetrated through. Riley pulled out cautiously, keeping the drill humming slowly as he went. I could feel the blood dripping off the side of my head, tickling my nearly numb flesh as it ran.

Riley had the bloody drill bit right in front of my face and I could see little flecks of my bone attached to its ridges.

My blood dripped from the edge and onto the floor.

When he pulled the drill out of my view, the Watcher was standing just behind him. I fought the urge to scream as it walked up to where I lay on the table and leaned over. Its skin was a demonic red, and I could see what looked to be snake-like parasites swimming just under its transparent flesh. Enormous eyes bulged out of its skull, almost giving me the feeling that they were about to pop out of its elongated head. As it studied me, it stretched its thin lips into a smile, exposing thorny, animal-like teeth.

"It's standing right next to you, isn't it?" Riley asked as he backed up, his eyes wide on his sweat-drenched face. "I thought I felt it."

Although the pain in my head was throbbing like an earthquake, and I could feel the hot blood dripping from my skull, I managed to say through clenched teeth, "Yes, it's right in front of me."

The Watcher placed his protracted fingers on the side of my head, inspecting the wound.

"Oh my God! He touched me!" I shrieked.

In the past, I had been unable to interact with the Watchers. Although I could see them, I was powerless to hear or touch them. Our latest experiment had placed me into their realm. As odd as it sounded, I now stood betwixt worlds.

It leaned in close, studying my face. It seemed to be perplexed that I was able to see it, and was trying to figure out why. I felt its slender finger gliding smoothly over the torn flesh on the side of my head, and then, to my horror, its finger slipped into the drilled hole. It penetrated slowly, traveling through my flesh almost sexually until I felt him touch the surface of my brain. The most overwhelming feeling of pain I had ever experienced caressed me like a lover—it was simply *glorious*.

The Watcher whispered something into my ear that I could not understand, sounding almost like a nest of bees had built a hive within the confines of my brain. I fell into unconsciousness before I could scream, half in pleasure, half in terror.

"Will, are you okay?" Riley asked as I came back into consciousness. My head still throbbed where the Watcher had penetrated me.

"It touched me, Riley," I said. My left eye was dry and sore. "Can you please give me some drops of Visine, please?"

As he gave me the eyedrops, I struggled to think of what it meant to exist in the same world as the Watchers.

"Do you see it now?" Riley asked, staring around the room even though he had never seen one himself.

I looked around weakly. My left eye had never been as good since I cut the eyelid off, though. "We're so close, Riley. I was standing in their world. I felt it touch me."

"You know, Will. Do you ever consider the fact that you might be hallucinating?"

I felt my anger rise. "Get the fuck out of my apartment."

Riley turned pale. "Listen—I go along with you, and I sort of believe in them too, but—"

"GET THE FUCK OUT!" I screamed, leaping up from the table. I held my hand over the hole in the side of my head to prevent blood from leaking out. I had taken some drugs to slow some of the leaking down, but it still ran thickly through my fingers.

"I'm not leaving," Riley said. "I'm your friend and you need me."

I glared at him, attempting to intimidate him, but he just returned my stare. "Riley, if you ever again go where you just took this conversation you can kiss our friendship goodbye and never speak to me again! The Watchers are real, godammit! Not only that, they threaten our very existence! We may be the only people on the whole planet that can stop them! Don't you want to see through this fucking veil that God has placed over our faces?"

For a brief moment, I actually heard what I sounded like and let my words sink into my brain.

Admittedly, I did sound like a total madman. It's just that, from the bottom of my soul, I feel they are real. That night, we sat around my kitchen table and discussed a way to get back into their world.

"We need to find a way that will allow me to stay there for a long period of time," I said, watching Riley intently as he sipped his coffee.

The next day, I found myself sitting in a kitchen chair, my teeth biting down into a thick piece of wood. I was quite terrified, as I knew what we were about to do could easily kill me. Riley was standing just to my left, a hammer gripped powerfully in his fist. In his palm were seven three-inch nails—seven being the number of the Lord. By having the nails in my head, I would be able to control the level of intensity with a push or pull of my fingers.

"You want to close your eyes?" Riley asked, placing the first nail on the top of my skull hesitantly. "I can put a cloth over your bad eye."

"I can't," I said, taking the wood out my mouth to speak. "I have to see the Watchers. In fact, if I pass out, you need to wake me up as soon as possible."

Riley hit the head of the nail delicately at first, and it only penetrated the flesh slightly.

"You're going to have to hit it a little harder," I said, noticing the way my voice trembled.

I could almost see a blurry ghost-like form of a Watcher just ahead. Soon, it would come into focus. I stuck the wood back between my teeth and waited, my heart fluttering in anticipation.

Riley brought the hammer up and hit the nail a little harder this time.

Pain exploded into my skull as the nail penetrated my deeper nerve endings. A single teardrop fell from my left eye and across my cheek and I moaned with a mix of sensual pleasure and deep agony. Just ahead I could see the incorporeal form of the Watcher gradually coming into focus.

"More?" Riley asked, his chalky face glowing with arousal for what he was doing to me.

I nodded, the muscles on my face twitching spasmodically. Although it was tremendously painful, it also left me feeling more exhilarated than I had ever remembered. I felt like a traveler going into a new and unexplored world. "Get those fucking nails into my skull, my friend," I moaned through my teeth. "Don't be afraid. This is fantastic!"

Riley put the face of the hammer against the nail that jutted out of my skull and brought it back ever so slightly. He then began to tap painstakingly, letting the nail sink into my skull. Each tap was a new explosion of agony, accompanied only by the feeling of sweet elation that I felt. It was like a perverse symphony of pain and inspiration.

There was a soft pop as the nail breached through the skull. I know it's impossible, but I could actually feel the head of the nail brushing up against my brain. It burned but in a good way.

Although the almost solid form of the Watcher was edged with lines of fuzziness, I could still see him quite well. He sat on the sofa, only feet away, as he watched us curiously. I don't think he realized that I could see him.

I bit deep down into the wood, my teeth beginning to ache as Riley moved to the second nail, then on to the third. Dark motes swam before my eyes, threatening to drag me into unconsciousness. By the time the seventh nail perforated the final layer of my skull, I had reached a level of intensity that could only be described as Zen. The nail pierced a little too deep, entering into my brain like a sliver of ice. I felt little spasms of energy travel like electrified insects down the base of my spine, and the nerves in my legs began to twitch spastically.

Spitting the piece of wood to the floor, I exhaled heavily. The flesh around my skull was throbbing with every beat of my heart. To think I once thought that I was almost incapable of feeling such pain.

The Watcher was no longer on the sofa, in fact he was nowhere to be seen. With a pang of fear, I realized that the pain threshold might not have been strong enough to thrust me within their world as I had hoped.

I ran my hand gently across my head, feeling the metal nails that were deeply embedded into my skull. I stood up, and then paused as waves of vertigo slammed into me.

"Will?" Riley asked, his voice high with panic.

"Yeah?" I turned around, only to be shown a sight so surreal that at first my pain numbed brain could not comprehend it.

I was still sitting in the chair before me, even though I was now standing. Like a ghost, I watched as Riley put his head to my chest and listened for a heartbeat. Trails of blood fell from the nails that protruded from my skull—giving me an appearance not unlike Jesus Christ, our savior. I watched with rising dread, realizing that my heart must have finally failed.

Behind my corpse was the most surreal thing that I had ever seen. The floor underneath Riley's blood splattered sneakers was nothing but black, star speckled space. What can only be described as a kaleidoscopic spider web hung in the air behind him, thousands of colors pulsing throughout the lines psychedelically. I could see the vague outlines of winged, bat-like men flying around the web, twirling around every time a new color would flash. I heard one howl mysteriously, and I felt my jaw drop open in awe.

"Oh my God," Riley whispered, staring down at my body with a stunned expression on his ugly face.

Much to my aversion, his eyes narrowed, and he looked down upon my corpse lasciviously. He began to lick the blood around the nails—his tongue darting out like a snake as his hand rubbed the crotch of my blood drenched jeans.

I slapped at him angrily, but my hand only sliced through him as if he was an illusion. We had gone too far, I no longer stood betwixt worlds. I looked away from Riley and his filthy tongue with disgust. In the last glimpse that I caught, he was plunging his tongue deep into the hole where we had drilled into only yesterday, removing the hardened blood with his fingernails.

When I heard the faint hissing behind me, I realized that I had entered the world of the Watcher. I could feel its hot breath crashing into the back of my head. I turned around tentatively, my mind preparing itself for what I would see.

It was standing only a few feet away, dissecting me with its protruding eyes. It pulled back its moist lips so languidly it seemed like a dream, exposing its needle filled mouth. Its eyes spun around in their sockets as it opened its jaws, long trails of saliva dripping from the razor sharp edges of its teeth. It held out its slender, wiry arm and wiggled its knife-like fingers back and forth like a sluggish crab.

I took a deep breath and closed my eyes in anticipation. I grinned—giving myself to what I knew was inevitable.

It detonated into me, seeming to glide through my flesh and internal organs with millions of razors, diving around through my body like a graceful swimmer. I rode with the pain, enjoying the breathtaking sensory overload like an explosive blood-soaked orgasm. For the first time in my existence, I felt truly *alive*. The last thought that entered my screaming brain before I ceased to exist, was how truly delightful the agony was.

WITH QUIET VIOLENCE

Melissa had already begun to melt. A pool of water ran from her tiny feet onto the wooden floor. Her five-year-old body stood rigid before the fireplace, hands held to her side like a statue, fingers blue and caked with crystals of ice. She wore the same white dress she'd worn in her coffin.

Michael's face looked haggard when he spoke, the face of a man hanging onto the edge of cliff by only his bloodied fingernails, eyes deadened with the resignation of his fate. "You aren't going to believe this, but I demanded that God give her to me. My faith was nearly gone."

I watched the water drop from Melissa onto the floor in soft *plunks*. A muffled ripping sound emitted from her body, a noise like her flesh was tearing apart under the ice. The firelight caused shadows to dance across her shiny face hypnotically.

"She came back to me, Richard," Michael said, his fingers running lovingly over her icy skin. "I can't believe it. God gave her back to me."

"You don't know that," I said, feeling repulsed by the dead girl. I noticed her eyes moved slightly. "We don't know what the hell this thing is. God doesn't give people back."

It was painful staring into the face of Michael O'Connor after he'd lost his little girl. When I looked into his eyes, I was always overwhelmed. They made me feel like I was staring into a window of a blazing house, watching someone burn to death—only the person was just standing there stoically letting the flames devour his blistering flesh.

"It's Melissa," he said. "She *is* from God, Richard. And don't call her a thing."

Looking at Michael by the flickering fire, his dead little girl standing before the flames, I could see the astonishing transformation. Gone were his pudgy chipmunk-like cheeks— replaced by sharp, severe cheekbones. The eyes, that at one time had twinkled with a mischievous gleam, were dark and gloomy, an edge of menace in the pupils, as if he had just crawled from the battlefield of a particularly brutal war. His frame was wiry and emaciated, nothing like the rotund form of only two years before. His hair, once full and curly, was shaved down to his scalp. Michael held the look of someone on the verge of shrieking in anguish before folding to the floor in a quivering fetal position.

Melissa died in a drowning accident. Only a year before that, his wife, Lisa, had died from an agonizingly slow bout with cancer. Melissa had always been a very special child, so wise for her years that it was frightening. When I first heard she was dead, I broke down and cried right where I stood.

We had gone to the cabin to escape Michael's grief, to get him away from all that reminded him of his lost little girl. I don't think he had left the state of Arkansas in his whole life, so I felt the change of scenery in the Pennsylvania mountains would do him good. Though being here had not erased his grief, he seemed more relaxed than I'd seen him in a long while.

We found her in the snow outside the cabin, standing rigidly in the cold wind. The moonlight made her blue skin shimmer like the stars above. Snowflakes swirled around her. I couldn't even breathe I was so stunned.

Michael wept instantly, starting with an odd, painful sob before exploding from his lips like a storm. He fell to his knees in the snow, shoulders shaking as he whispered his daughter's name like a mantra.

We carried her heavy body into the cabin, my mind too numb and unable to grasp the possibility of a dead girl coming back to see her daddy.

"Don't you realize how strange this is? How impossible?"

As I asked the question, a large piece of ice fell from Melissa's open mouth to the floor, shattering into tiny slivers.

She spoke, water dripping from her glossy teeth, though

her lips never formed the words. "Daddy, I'm sorry I went swimming without your permission," the child's voice said, all wet and soggy, almost bubbly, as it boomed from still lips.

My skin prickled. It was too surreal, like demonic possession.

Michael sobbed before he was able to speak. "I know, honey. I know."

Melissa began to cry. Her eyes slithered slowly to the left until they locked with mine, the sound of ice being dragged against stone as they moved. She had no pupils—just the dead blackness of space. I moved backwards as if struck, her dark gaze piercing into me with quiet violence.

"That's not Melissa," I whispered, my breath stopping as her eyes stabbed into me again with frightening rage.

Michael hissed—his fists curling up into tightly clenched balls. "She came back to me. God knew how much I needed her and He gave her back to me."

I ignored the sound of the ice breaking as she melted free. "Melissa is dead."

"Don't you think I know that!" He snapped, grabbed my shoulders and pulled me into him, spraying my face with spittle. "I've suffered every fucking day since she died, Richard! Not a day goes by that I don't hear the sound of her laughter! See her running by in the corner of my eye! I see her every night in my sleep! Not a day goes by that I don't feel the loss of her!"

"Listen to yourself, Michael. You just said it. Melissa *is* dead. You're talking about her in the past tense because you know this. Dead people don't come back."

He fell to his knees before the frozen corpse. I watched, repulsed, as Melissa's eyes crept sluggishly downward.

His voice dropped to a soft whisper. "I prayed every day for her to come back to me…and now she's here. There is no other way to see this except for an act of God."

Her blue-pink fingers wiggled back and forth, water dripping from the edge of her nails. Her eyes darted back to me, daring me to speak against her.

"People don't come back from the dead," I said. "Whatever the hell this thing is, it's not Melissa. Any fool can feel that she's dangerous."

"Fuck you," he hissed, wrapping his arms around her icy corpse, his hot tears falling onto glacial arms with a soft hiss. The little girl giggled, her throat undulating softly under her motionless mouth as if there were insects awakening from within her cold flesh.

Michael flinched when she giggled like that, his body tensing.

I think some part of him knew that what he was embracing was just plain wrong, but he was desperate. Hell, if I had been in his place, I would have done the same damn thing.

By the next morning, Melissa had completely thawed out. She moved sluggishly, with a clumsy jerking of her limbs—like she didn't have the ability to walk on her own and someone above was pulling invisible strings in lurching motions. Michael watched her with the guilty gaze of a heroin addict—a man who knew the absolute wickedness of what he was doing, but was unable to stop.

The snow had never really let up, and continued to blanket the world around us. Its usual serene beauty no longer made me feel safe.

She had no memory of anything after she'd died; she remembered only up to the point where she had drowned. At one point, they sang a childhood lullaby; Melissa perched awkwardly on his lap, a line of pinkish drool falling from her slack mouth. Her voice sounded far off, as if she were talking from a long distance away and was using her body as a receptacle.

It was one of the most frightening things I have ever witnessed, and to this day, when I see that moment in my mind, I'm gripped by a wave of revulsion unlike anything else I've ever experienced.

Because it was also the first time I noticed she was decomposing.

Melissa's skin was turning slightly gray—no longer the pale white color of the snow she seemed born of. Her eyes, at first filled with moisture, had grown hard and black, not unlike the eyes of a doll. They did not focus on anything, only stared into nowhere, and I was certain that if I touched them, they would feel like coal.

"Her skin is rotting," I said, no longer concerned with treading lightly.

Michael ignored me, picked her up, and took her into the bathroom. A few moments later, I followed and watched from the doorway. I could only shake my head and fight the urge to weep. Michael had a tube of ointment and was rubbing it over her festering wounds; desperately trying to stop what he knew was coming.

Melissa just stared at me, her dark mouth like a third eye. Tear tracks glistened down Michael's face as he mumbled, his hands frantically massaging the medicine into her sores.

"It hurts, Daddy," Melissa said, her voice soft and vulnerable—yet more distant than ever.

Michael closed his tear-filled eyes. "I know, honey. I'm trying to make it better."

"I'm sorry, Michael," I whispered.

"I don't understand," he said. "Why is God taking her back? She's dying."

Though I tried to hold it back, I gasped—the air fleeing my body as if from a punch.

He was rubbing the ointment onto her bare back, the strap of her dress hanging limply to the side. Her spine was sticking through the rotted flesh, yet his fingers rubbed lovingly over the knobs of bone.

"She was never alive," I said, part of me hoping to destroy the abomination before me.

"He's taking her back," he said distantly. His fingers stroked her protruding spine obsessively. "He gave her to me to strengthen my faith, but now He's punishing me for questioning Him."

"If God gave her to you, He's a cruel God."

Michael buried his head into his daughter's chest. "Leave us alone, please."

"I love you, Daddy," Melissa said as I walked away. Her voice was far away and creepy, like a tape player with a low battery.

By the next day, the skin on her cheek had rotted away completely, exposing her cheekbone to the stale cabin air.

Maggots could be seen eating the flesh on a wound in her forearm. Melissa could no longer speak, only moan softly in a queer sing-song-like melody.

Michael continued to frantically rub her with ointment.

I cried as I watched them, wanting so badly to do something—anything—to stop the pain my friend was feeling, but I was helpless. We both were. By this time I was too far-gone to help, too numb.

Melissa's face had begun to sink, the outline of her skull beginning to take shape under her decaying skin. It was as if her bones were coming through, her flesh melting away like ice.

Later that night, the wind pounding the walls of the cabin, Michael spoke to me for the last time. "I'm going with her, Richard. I can't bear to lose her again. You've been very good to me. I'll always love you for that."

We embraced. Sometimes I can still feel his warm arms around me, and to this day I wish I had stopped him.

Michael picked up Melissa, who dangled like a rag doll, arms and legs swinging lifelessly as they moved. He did not look back when he opened the door and walked into the brutal wind.

I watched him carry his little girl into the sea of white, his dark clothing stark against the swirling snow, until he disappeared, the whiteness devouring him languidly.

When they found his body several days later, Melissa was not with him. He was leaned against a tree, his arms circled around nothing in a dead embrace.

Not a day has passed that I don't think about what happened to us at the cabin. Part of me often wonders if we both didn't suffer from some bizarre hallucination—or if I had somehow bought into Michael's fantasy of bringing his girl back to life.

I often think of them.

Even outside of sleep, I can still hear Melissa's laughter with vivid clarity—see Michael weeping over her decomposing body. My dreams have become infected by my experience that winter. I haven't had a good sleep in at least a year.

I dread the upcoming winter.

It seems I am never truly warm—no matter how many

sweaters I put on. Often, I wake up in the middle of the night shivering beside my wife, my teeth chattering together.

I have my own little girl now, and I can't help but think of the cabin when I look into her beautiful eyes. Knowing what happened to Melissa has tainted the elegance of my child. She seems so fragile now, her life so fleeting, and it's not hard to imagine myself in Michael's place.

I hope my friend and his daughter have found some peace— wherever they are.

I know I haven't.

FEELING KATHERINE

Looking deep into the whites of her frightened eyes, Simon felt something for the first time in over a decade. It tickled at his brain, skirting across in playful, almost painful, little steps.

As soon as he realized the feeling was love, he knew Katherine had to die.

"Simon, don't do this," she said, her voice trembling with each whispery word.

Simon could tell she had read his mind, and once again he was struck with a profound fear. He had killed dozens of women, but none had touched him in the way Katherine had. It was as if she had her delicate fingers probing right into his black psyche. In the past, he hadn't felt even an inkling of guilt when he brought his knife to a woman's flesh—sometimes he even smiled at them, watching his reflection in their eyes as they exhaled their last breath.

"I told you to stop talking to me," Simon said, hating the guttural sound of his own voice. "Your manipulations are so fucking transparent."

"I know you feel something, Simon. I can see it in your eyes."

He studied her soft, doll-like face, inhaling deeply as if he could somehow devour her soul through the air. Katherine sat handcuffed to her chair, her expressive eyes pleading. Part of him wanted to run his fingers through her blonde hair, but he knew it was dangerous. Doing that had only made him more attached to her, something he instinctively knew was dangerous.

He wanted to tell her she was right, but instead he said, "I told you not to call me by my first name. If you do it again, I will kill you. Don't push me, Katherine."

He had kept her alive longer than any other victim. Most of them stayed here in his basement for only a few days at most. Katherine had been his captive for two months now.

She had listened to him attentively as he told her of his constant struggle to control his violent compulsions. It had come to the point where she had practically become his therapist, nodding sadly as he told tale after tale of his victim's struggles. He had watched the tears run down her face when he talked about the brutal beatings he had received as a child. As soon as he realized she had begun to understand and empathize with him, it terrified him to the very core of his rotting soul.

Katherine had also told him stories of her own life, each one drenched with pain and sadness. He found himself nodding at her, feeling as if they were made to be together. Every time a thought of this kind came to him—the belief he could somehow have a normal life with her—it left him feeling wrathful. Every night he struggled with the puzzle of why this provoked anger in him, and the mystery eluded him, hiding itself deep in his troubled mind.

He knew he was deeply in love with her, though; that was a fact of which he was certain.

"Just let me touch you, Si—," she stopped, realizing by the predatory way he cocked his bald head to the side that she may have pushed him too far. "Take these handcuffs off of my hands."

He shook his head. "I can't do that. And I noticed you almost said my name. You are standing at the edge of one very precarious fucking cliff, my dear. Don't make me launch you off."

Katherine nodded and looked down, mocking as if she was staring over the edge of his proverbial cliff. "Damn, there are a lot of bodies down there."

Simon smiled, despite the fact she was ridiculing him. Katherine had a way of doing this that somehow didn't make him angry, and it was one of the reasons he found himself so helplessly in love with her. "There you go again. You are either certifiably insane or courageous as hell."

Katherine grinned, breaking his heart with her dazzling

smile. "My father used to say it was a little bit of both." She paused momentarily, watching him almost affectionately. "You just know I'm going to bring this up again."

He ran his fingers over his smooth scalp and tried not to smile. "I'm not letting you go. We both know that I can't."

She sighed. "I know you won't kill me and we both know that you can't keep me locked down in this basement forever. You're just going to have to learn to trust me."

"I can't do that." He found himself touching her hair, reveling in its softness, imagining that she enjoyed the way it felt. "There is no way you will be able to keep quiet about your little stay here. It's impossible."

She leaned to the side, letting his fingers drag through her hair. Although part of him wanted to think that she really had feelings for him, he knew she was merely trying to manipulate him.

"Simon," Katherine said.

He pulled back as if burned—clenching the knife tightly in his shaking fist as he stared down at her, a slow, dark smile forming under his long nose. "I warned you."

She snapped at him ferociously, her eyes wild. "Simon, I know you have feelings for me, Goddammit! Stop trying to hold yourself back!"

He sighed, his haunted eyes disappearing into the shadows of his face. "You have no idea how deeply I care for you. Every night I dream that you might actually have feelings for me, Katherine. And every night I wake up to the cold reality that I keep you locked up in this basement."

"If you have real feelings for me, you will let me go."

"Can you honestly say you would have even acknowledged my existence if I hadn't taken you? If I had asked for a date in the real world, you would have laughed in my face."

"How do you know this? I do have feelings for you, Simon, despite the fact that I am being held captive in your basement. And you have no idea what I would have done had you asked me for a date instead of taking me like this."

"You are a liar. I'm a monster and we both know this. I am not worthy of love and I am incapable of redemption. You say these things because you know I want to hear them."

"To know anyone completely is to know they are worthy of some kind of love. Redemption is always possible."

Simon laughed, each breath escaping his lips in furious hisses. "That is so fucking trite. Do you really think I can be manipulated this easily?" He leaned down, until he could see fear deep in her beautiful blue eyes. "I have skinned alive women who looked just like you, Katherine." He ran the backs of his fingers over the delicate skin of her cheek. "I have bit into the flesh of these women, enjoying the way their body would explode in pain, loving the way they screamed as I tore away their skin with my teeth. I have set women afire, admiring the way they can still shriek when their head is burning in flames— their skin blistering." He leaned closer, letting his teeth drag across the bridge of her nose—he stopped when his eyes were only inches from hers. "You have the fucking audacity to tell me I am worthy of love? That I am capable of redemption? And expect me to fucking believe it?"

"I do believe it," she whispered. "And I do care about you, Simon."

"Don't fucking say my name. I am not going to say this again."

"Simon, you can't scare me anymore. We both know you are never going to hurt me."

He launched the knife forward, burying it deeply into her chest, stopping only when his knuckles sunk into her flesh. He flinched as the hot blood splattered onto his clenched teeth, filling his mouth with her bitter taste. He stared into her eyes, feeling repulsive for the first time as he watched himself in her stunned expression. Her heartbeat reverberated through the knife and into the bones of his hand.

Katherine exhaled sharply, her breath slicing through the air twice before it stopped cold. Thick veins had snaked up her neck and into her temples.

Simon did not realizing he was crying until the first warm teardrop landed on the back of his hand and mixed with her blood.

"I love you, Katherine Mayer," he whispered.

He let go of the knife and fell to his knees, screaming loudly in the closed confines of his dark basement. He felt a warm trickling on his left knee and looked down to see her blood as it ran around him, oozing forward in slow motion.

Burying her body was difficult.

As she lay in the shallow ditch, the moonlight lighting up her face like some perverse, yet beautiful painting, he found himself longing once again for her smile. Hardening himself, he threw a shovel full of dirt into her face and moaned. When he realized he was whispering her name like a mantra, he became furious, stabbing the shallow grave with the shovel, feeling sick when he heard the crunching of her broken teeth.

Never again will I allow myself to grow so close to one of my victims, he thought to himself as he stared up at the skull-like moon.

He felt invisible again, and enjoyed it. Katherine had somehow begun to make him feel naked and vulnerable.

As soon as he arrived back at his house, he began the tedious process of cleaning the basement. The blood-covered chair sat in the center of the room, a grisly reminder of what he had done. He leaned down and touched the thick puddle of congealed blood and studied the crimson tip of his finger. Closing his eyes, he touched the finger to his tongue, savoring her one final time.

As the taste of her blood filled his mouth, an image of Katherine detonated into his mind. Her blood-covered face was down, though her eyes were locked on his. A ghostly smile erupted underneath her nose and she began to giggle mockingly. Repulsed, he spit her blood to the ground, wiping his finger off on his jeans.

Simon felt she had somehow invaded him in that moment, he had felt her presence so profoundly he could almost smell her scent. He could still hear her giggling in his brain.

Feeling a desperate need to rid himself of her presence, he retreated upstairs into a hot shower. As he washed himself vigorously, the soap lathered around his body like a protective shield, he kept itching at his wrist. When he noticed the hard lump just under the flesh, he stood rigid, as if the water had suddenly turned icy cold.

He stepped out of the shower slowly, rubbing at the lump on his wrist. The itching was maddening and he was suddenly struck with the intense feeling that a beetle of some kind had managed to bury itself underneath his skin. It was not attached to his bone, but instead rolled around loosely, turning around under his flesh like a parasite.

He thought he heard a brief, feminine titter in his head, but it was gone as quickly as it had danced through.

Two minutes later, he found himself standing before his steam covered mirror, his knife clutched in his fist as he studied the large, pebble sized lump.

He wiped the mirror and looked upon his chiseled face.

When he saw another lump set just above his right eyebrow, he had to chase the scream that threatened to erupt from his throat back into his mind. Feeling himself shiver in disgust, he examined lump on his forehead. Just like the one on his wrist, it felt loose underneath his flesh and moved slightly. When he touched it, he was hit with a gnawing pain.

Simon placed the sharp edge of the blade against his wrist and began to cut, warily trying to avoid a vein. Blood splattered into the sink, providing a stark contrast to the white porcelain. He cut a thin line just near the lump and then pushed his thumb against the pebble-sized pocket in his flesh.

A single tooth tore through the wound and landed in the sink with an audible *click*.

Simon stared down at the blood-covered incisor and felt his stomach retch. When he realized the very same thing might be residing in his forehead, he had to fight the urge to claw away the flesh with his nails.

With the experience of a surgeon, he sliced a neat line just underneath the protruding gob on his forehead, leaned forward, and pushed yet another tooth from his skin.

A thin line of blood dripped from the newly acquired wound, running just across his eye and down his cheek like a teardrop. Unable to fight his disgust, he leaned forward and vomited. He shrieked when he saw he had regurgitated at least six more teeth, many of them still holding the root. Frantically, he began to run his hands over his nude body in a desperate search for more of the horrifying lumps.

Not wanting to cover his flesh with clothes, he lay in his bedroom and tried to meditate. It was something he often did when he felt overwhelmed.

Someone giggled. Simon sat up, his eyes wide underneath his still bleeding forehead.

"Katherine," he whispered, staring around the room. The only sound was the rustling of his curtains from the nighttime breeze.

He lay back on the bed, enjoying the cool air as it blew across his chest. Simon wondered if he had been hallucinating. He knew that Katherine's death had affected him on levels he still did not understand.

In the past, he had enjoyed the immense feeling of power he had derived from killing his victims. He enjoyed killing women, sighing in almost sexual pleasure in their final moments. This feeling of omnipotence was one of the reasons he kept killing so compulsively, it was a desperate need to recapture a moment when he felt like...somebody. They would not dare to laugh at him in such moments, it was a feeling he needed like food.

Katherine made him feel different. For the first time in his life he had felt as if he was no longer invisible. She looked into his eyes and verified that he was a human being, worthy of attention. That verification had left him defenseless, something he had never felt before.

He awoke to the wings of an insect fluttering on his chest. It felt as if a butterfly was flapping rapidly just underneath his left nipple, tickling his skin.

He touched his chest, running his fingers over his flesh with delicate precision. He knew what it was as soon it touched the edge of his forefinger and he rushed into the bathroom to get a better look at it in the fluorescent lighting.

A single eye stared at him from his chest. It blinked once, tickling him yet again, and continued to watch him. He knew as soon as he made eye contact with it, that it was Katherine.

He noticed just a sliver of an opening in the other side of his chest and saw with abhorrence that it was yet another eye. He could see a pupil moving around just under the slit, giving him the sick feeling that a bug had delved a deep nest into his flesh and was using it as a home.

Just the tip of a nose could be seen just below, followed by the ghostly outline of a set of full lips. He pushed at the lips with his fingers, pulling back suddenly when he felt what he knew could only be a tongue brushing against the still sealed flesh.

He picked up the blood-covered knife and held it to the eye. "Katherine, this must end now. If I have to, I will literally cut you from my flesh."

As he watched, the sensual lips bloomed just above his belly button like an obscene flower, forming into a wide, wicked grin. Some of the teeth were missing from the smile.

"Hello, Simon," Katherine said, the eye staring into his, daring him to look away.

Simon felt a hollow sensation in his body from where the mouth spoke—the sound of her voice rumbling through his skin and into his skull with maddening echoes.

"Get out of me," he whispered. "I promise you, I will stick this blade right into your fucking eye."

Katherine giggled hysterically and locked her eye onto the end of the knife. A line of blood dripped from her mouth and down his waist.

"Are you sure I am real, Simon?" she asked. "How do you know that I'm not just a product of your sick fuck mind?"

Simon reached down, picked up one her teeth and held it before his chest. "This looks real enough to me."

"I can read your thoughts, you know," she said, laughing again. "I did love you, Simon. I know it makes me sick, shows I must have had all kinds of problems. But I did love you. At first I was repulsed, but something happened. I wanted to protect you. I wanted to save you."

He almost fell backwards, as if struck. "You are lying."

"Why would I lie Simon?" she asked. "I loved you. As disturbing as it sounds, I loved you. You have no idea how much. I would have given up my other life. I would have helped you fight your compulsions."

"Shut up," he whispered, placing the edge of the blade even

closer to her eye. "I swear, I will take it out."

"Do you honestly think you can scare me now? You already buried me in a shallow grave."

"You didn't care about me," he muttered, his voice dropping to a weak whisper.

She laughed uproariously. "I would have spent the rest of my life with you. I wanted you. I would have done anything. The only reason I didn't tell you was because I knew you would not believe me. I hoped that our relationship would develop."

He set the tip of the blade into the eye, causing her to explode into even more fits of laughter. Stabbing into his chest, he punctured the eyeball, surprising himself at the blast of pain he felt.

"No one ever loved you and no one ever will. Just me. You killed the only person who could have loved you. I can see by your thoughts you fear and know this, Simon. You will never find that again."

"Shut the fuck up!" he howled, sticking his finger through the slit in the other eye, tearing away at the flesh as blood splattered into the mirror.

"I loved you!"

Simon shrieked and plunged the knife into her mouth, sending a fountain of blood into the already drenched mirror. The eruption of pain in his stomach blossomed as he pushed the knife even deeper. She continued to laugh as he stabbed her mouth, teeth falling out of his stomach and onto the hard linoleum floor.

He fell back against the wall and slid down slowly, unable to breathe as his life fluids streamed out of her mutilated mouth in waves. The mouth continued to laugh, the blood spewing out like vomit.

"I loved you too," he whispered before he died, her bubbling laughter still ringing in his ears like a blood-soaked aria.

ABOUT THE AUTHOR

David Whitman is the author of several books, including HARLAN, DEADFEL-LAS, and BODY COUNTING. He is also the co-author of SCARY REDNECKS AND OTHER INBRED HORRORS and APPALACHIAN GALAPAGOS: A SCARY RED-NECKS COLLECTION with Weston Ochse.

David's short fiction has been published in over 100 publications over the last fif-teen years, including several honorable mentions in Ellen Datlow's and Terry Windling's YEAR'S BEST FANTASY AND HORROR.

Future projects include the sequel DEADFELLAS 2: ONE STEP BEYOND and other projects, including a new novel and a possible movie adaptation of DEADFELLAS.

He lives in northeastern Pennsylvania with his son Miles.

Curious about other Crossroad Press books?
Stop by our site:
http://store.crossroadpress.com
We offer quality writing
in digital, audio, and print formats.

Enter the code FIRSTBOOK
to get 20% off your first order from our store!
Stop by today!